£8.99

PRAISE FOR *LITTLE EYES*

LONGLISTED FOR THE BOOKER INTERNATIONAL PRIZE 2020
A *GUARDIAN* & *TIMES* BEST NOVEL OF 2020

'Ingenious… An artful exploration of solitude and empathy in a globalised world… In a nimble, fast-moving narrative, what's most impressive is the way she foregrounds her characters' inner hopes and fears.'   *Guardian*

'Disturbing… Schweblin enjoys hovering just above the normal. Inspired by Samuel Beckett, she is interested in exposing absurdities.'

Financial Times

'This has a propulsive, Dave Eggers-ish readability.'   *Daily Mail*

'*Little Eyes* makes for masterfully uneasy reading; it's a book that burrows under your skin.'   *Telegraph*

'Wonderfully chilly, astute and borderline-horrific.'

Sunday Times, Best Sci-fi Books of the Year, 2020

'I cannot remember a book so efficient in establishing character and propelling narrative; there's material for a hundred novels in these deft, rich 242 pages… The writing, ably translated from the Spanish by Megan McDowell, is superb, fully living up to the promise of Schweblin's stunning previous novel, *Fever Dream*… A slim volume as expansive and ambitious as an epic.'

New York Times

'In Samanta Schweblin's fiendishly readable *Little Eyes* the new must-have tech gadget allows users to leapfrog into the lives of strangers – a sharp idea that became even more pertinent with the isolation and atomisation of lockdown.'

Guardian, Best Fiction of the Year, 2020

'A timely meditation on humanity and technology.'   *Harper's Bazaar*

'*Little Eyes* acts as a clear ⸱⸱⸱⸱⸱⸱ ⸱⸱ make has consequences… It does fe⸱⸱

D1347647

'Deftly translated by Megan McDowell, *Little Eyes* succeeds through its depiction of a world that is profoundly human... In a globalized world where technology claims to have erased frontiers and within which the transnational market heralds empty promises of economic equality, *Little Eyes* provides us with a powerful examination of the underlining disparities that persist.'

Times Literary Supplement

'Enjoyable reading... Riffing on everyday human foibles – jealousy, capriciousness, existential restlessness...the understatedly arch tone is well served by Megan McDowell's translation, which is so slick that one hardly seems to be reading a translated work.'

Literary Review

'If you want a spookily prescient vision of human isolation both assuaged and deepened by inscrutable, glitch-prone tech, then *Little Eyes* more than fits the brief... Adroitly served by Megan McDowell's winningly deadpan translation, these stories deal not in 'truly brutal plots' but 'desperately human and quotidian' urges, fears and scams... In the middle of our stay-at-home, broadband-enabled apocalypse, that feels right.'

Spectator

'The 'toys' Schweblin has created are the perfect hybrid between a pet and a social network, enabling her to dissect problems that touch all of our lives: the dark side of the internet; the global epidemic of loneliness; the dumb inertia that leads us to jump on board with the latest trend... As always in the worlds Schweblin creates, the real monsters are to be found not in the outside world, but inside each of us.'

New York Times (Spanish edition)

'This brilliant and disturbing book resembles Margaret Atwood's *Handmaid's Tale* in how it speculates... Schweblin unspools a disquieting portrait of the dark sides of connectivity and the kinds of animalistic cyborgs it can make of us, as we walk through barriers that even spirits cannot cross.'

Literary Hub

'A nuanced exploration of anonymous connection and distant intimacy in our heavily accessible yet increasingly isolated lives... Capacious, touching, and disquieting, this is not-so-speculative fiction for an overnetworked and underconnected age.'

Kirkus

PRAISE FOR *FEVER DREAM*

'A book to read in one sitting – bold, uncanny and utterly gripping.'

Observer, Best Fiction of 2017

'A nauseous, eerie read, sickeningly good.'

Emma Cline, bestselling author of *The Girls*

'Transcends the sensational plot elements to achieve a powerful and humane vision.' *Financial Times*, Best Books of 2017

'A gloriously creepy fable.' *Guardian*, Best Fiction of 2017

'Dazzling, unforgettable, and deeply strange. I've never read anything like it.'

Evening Standard, Books of the Year, 2017

'Mesmerizing.' *Washington Post*

'Read this in a single sitting and by the end I could hardly breathe. It's a total mind-wrecker. Amazing. Thrilling.'

Max Porter, author of *Grief is the Thing with Feathers* & *Lanny*

'Punches far above its weight… The sort of book that makes you look under the bed last thing at night and sleep with the light on.'

Daily Mail

'Subtle, dreamy and indelibly creepy.'

Economist, Best Books of 2017

'The genius of *Fever Dream* is less in what it says than in how Schweblin says it, with a design at once so enigmatic and so disciplined that the book feels as if it belongs to a new literary genre altogether.' *The New Yorker*

LITTLE EYES
SAMANTA SCHWEBLIN

**TRANSLATED BY
MEGAN McDOWELL**

ONEWORLD

A Oneworld Book

First published in Great Britain, the Republic of Ireland and Australia
by Oneworld Publications, 2020
This paperback edition published 2021

Originally published in Spanish, and in a slightly different form,
as *Kentukis* by Literatura Random House, Barcelona in 2018
Published by arrangement with Riverhead Books, an imprint of Penguin Publishing Group,
a division of Penguin Random House LLC

Copyright © 2018, 2020 by Samanta Schweblin
English translation copyright © 2020 by Megan McDowell

The moral right of Samanta Schweblin to be identified as the
Author of this work has been asserted by her in accordance with the Copyright,
Designs and Patents Act 1988

ISBN 978-1-78607-861-2
eISBN 978-1-78607-793-6

Printed and bound in Great Britain by Clays Ltd, Elcograf S.p.A.

This is a work of fiction. While, as in all fiction, the literary perceptions and insights are
based on experience, all names, characters, places, and incidents either are products of
the author's imagination or are used fictitiously.

Excerpt from *The Left Hand of Darkness* by Ursula K. Le Guin, published in
Great Britain in 2017 by Gollancz, an imprint of the Orion Publishing Group.
Used by permission of the Orion Publishing Group.

Oneworld Publications
10 Bloomsbury Street
London WC1B 3SR
United Kingdom

Stay up to date with the latest books,
special offers, and exclusive content from
Oneworld with our newsletter

Sign up on our website
oneworld-publications.com

MIX
Paper from
responsible sources
FSC® C018072
www.fsc.org

Before starting the engine, make sure people are clear of the danger area.

Digger safety manual, 2018

Will you tell us about the other worlds out among the stars—the other kinds of men, the other lives?

Ursula K. Le Guin, THE LEFT HAND OF DARKNESS

South Bend

· ·

THE FIRST THING they did was show their tits. The three of them sat on the edge of the bed facing the camera, took off their shirts, and one by one, removed their bras. Robin had almost nothing to show but she did it anyway, paying more attention to the looks she got from Katia and Amy than to the game itself. If you want to survive in South Bend, she'd heard the girls say once, you have to make friends with the strong.

The animal's camera was installed behind its eyes, and sometimes it spun around on the three wheels hidden in its base, moving forward or backward. Someone was controlling the creature from somewhere else, and they didn't know who it was. The animal looked like a simple and artless plush panda bear, though really it was more similar to a football with one end sliced off so it could stand upright. Whoever was on the other side of the camera was trying to follow them without missing a thing, so Amy picked up the panda and put it on a chair so it would be right at the height of their tits. The gadget was Robin's, but everything Robin had was also Katia's and Amy's: that was the blood pact they had made on Friday, the pact that would join them together for the rest of their lives. And now they each had to do their own little show, so they got dressed again.

Amy put the animal back on the floor, picked up the bucket she'd brought from the kitchen, and placed it upside down over the panda. The bucket moved nervously, blindly, around the room. It collided with notebooks, shoes, and clothing strewn on the floor, which seemed to make it grow more desperate. Amy started to pant and let out excited moans, and the bucket stopped moving. Katia joined in the game, and they acted out a long and profound simultaneous orgasm.

"That doesn't count as your show," Amy warned Katia as soon as they managed to stop laughing.

"Of course not," said Katia, and she darted out of the room. "Get ready!" she cried as she ran down the hall.

Robin didn't usually feel all that comfortable with these games, though she admired Katia's and Amy's nerve, and the way they talked to boys, and how they managed to keep their hair always smelling good and their nails perfectly painted. When the games crossed certain lines, Robin wondered if they might not be testing her. She'd been the last one to join the "club," as they called themselves, and she tried hard to be worthy.

Katia returned to the room with her backpack. She sat down in front of the bucket and freed the panda.

"Pay attention," she said, looking at the camera, and the bear's eyes followed her.

Robin wondered if it could understand them. It seemed to hear them perfectly well, and they were speaking English, which is what everyone speaks. Maybe speaking English was the only good thing about having been born in a city as terribly boring as South Bend.

Katia opened her backpack, took out her yearbook, and looked for the class photo. Amy clapped and shouted:

"You brought the little whore? You're gonna show him?"

Katia nodded. She flipped the pages eagerly, the tip of her tongue poking out between her lips. When she found the girl she was looking for, she opened the album wide and held the photo in front of the bear. Robin peered over the book to see. It was Susan, the weird girl from her biology class that the club bullied for fun.

"They call her Big Ass," said Katia. She pursed her lips a couple of times, the way she did whenever she was about to do some high-level mischief, which was what being a member of the club demanded. "I'm going to show you how to make some free money with her," Katia told the camera. "Robin, darling, could you hold the book while I show the gentleman his job?"

Robin went over and held the book, unsure. Amy looked on curiously; she didn't know Katia's plan either. Katia scrolled through her phone until she found a video, and then she held the screen up in front of the bear's eyes. In the video, Susan lowered her stockings and underpants. It seemed to be filmed from the floor of the school bathroom, inside a stall; maybe the camera had been set up between the trash can and the wall. They heard some farts, and the three of them rolled with laughter, and they cried out in pleasure when, before flushing, Susan stood looking down at her own shit.

"This chick is loaded, my dear," said Katia. "Half for you

and the other half for us. It's just that the club can't blackmail her again, the teachers already have their eyes on us."

Robin didn't know what they were talking about, but it wasn't the first time the club hadn't included her in its most illegal activities. Soon Katia's show would be over and it would be her turn, and she hadn't thought of anything. Her hands were sweating. Katia took out her notebook and a pen and wrote down some information.

"Here's Big Ass's full name, phone number, e-mail, and mailing address," she said as she held up the notebook alongside the photo.

"And just how is our little guy going to get us our share of the money?" Amy asked Katia, winking at the camera and the presumed man behind it. Katia hesitated. "We don't know who the hell he is," said Amy. "That's why we showed him our tits, right?

Katia looked at Robin, as if asking her for help. It was in those brief moments that they counted on her, when Katia and Amy reached the heights of their individual rapaciousness and went to war with each other.

"How is the gentleman going to give us his e-mail, huh?" Amy went on, mocking Katia's plan.

"I know how," said Robin.

They both looked at her in surprise.

This would be her show, she thought, this was how she would emerge unscathed from the situation. The panda also turned toward her, trying to follow what was happening. Robin put the book down, went to her wardrobe, and opened a few drawers. She came back with a Ouija board that she opened and set down on the floor.

"Get on," she said to the animal.

And the bear did. The three plastic wheels on its base easily maneuvered onto the cardboard; it moved across the length of the alphabet, as if investigating. Though its body took up more than one letter at a time, soon enough they understood which one it was pointing at, hidden between its wheels. The bear settled in under the arch of the alphabet and waited. It apparently knew exactly how to use a Ouija board. Robin wondered what she would do when the other girls left and she was alone again with this bear, now that she'd shown it her tits and had taught it a way to communicate with her.

"Awesome," said Amy.

And Robin's mouth twisted into a smile.

"Which of the three of us do you think has the best tits?" asked Katia.

The bear moved quickly over the board's letters.

THEBLOND

Katia smiled proudly, clearly aware it was true.

How had she not thought of the Ouija board trick sooner? Robin wondered. She'd had the bear in her room for over a week, rolling around aimlessly. She could have talked calmly with him; maybe he was someone special, a boy she could have fallen in love with, and now she was ruining everything by letting Katia and Amy take over.

"Do you accept the deal with Big Ass?" asked Katia, showing him the photo of Susan once more.

The bear moved, started to write again.

WHORES

Robin frowned. She felt hurt, although maybe the bear's insult spoke well of him: she knew what they were doing wasn't right. Katia and Amy looked at each other and smiled proudly, stuck their tongues out at the bear.

"How crude," said Amy. "Let's see, what else does the gentleman have to say to us?"

"Yeah, what else are we, my little dildo?" Katia egged him on, blowing him sensual kisses with her hand. "What else would you like us to be?"

YOUTHREE

They had to concentrate to follow the words.

WILLPAYME

The three of them looked at one another.

TITSRECORDED400PERTITIS2400DOLLARS

Amy and Katia looked at each other a few seconds and burst out laughing. Robin was clutching her shirt, squeezing hard, struggling to force a smile.

"And who exactly is going to pay you, huh?" Amy asked, and pretended to be about to lift up her shirt again.

OTHERWISETITSTOSUSANSEMAIL

For the first time, Amy and Katia got serious. Robin couldn't decide whose side she should take; maybe her panda bear was a vigilante.

"You can send them to whoever you want," said Amy. "We have the best tits in the city. Nothing to be ashamed of."

Robin knew that didn't include her. Amy and Katia high-fived. Then the bear started to dance over the board, writing nonstop, spelling words that Robin could barely manage to read.

IHAVEVIDEOSROBINSMOTHERSHITTINGANDROBINSSISTERMASTURBATINGX6

It took concentration to follow letter by letter, but they couldn't look away.

FATHERSAYINGTHINGSTOMAID

Amy and Katia were watching the bear's dance in fascination, patient as they waited for each new humiliation.

ROBINNAKEDANDROBINTALKINGSHITABOUTAMYONTHEPHONE

Amy and Katia looked at each other. Then they looked at Robin, and they weren't smiling now.

ROBINPRETENDINGTOBEAMYANDTOBEKATIAANDTOKISSTHEM

The bear went on writing, but Amy and Katia stopped reading. They got up, gathered their things, and stormed out, slamming the door.

Trembling, while the bear kept moving over the board, Robin tried to figure out how the hell to turn the thing off. It didn't have a switch—she'd already noticed that—and in her desperation she couldn't find any other solution. She picked it up and tried to open the base with the point of a pair of scissors. The bear spun its wheels in an attempt to escape, but it was helpless. Robin couldn't find any crack to pry open, so she returned the bear to the floor and it went straight back to the board. Robin kicked it off. The bear squealed and she cried out—she didn't know it could make noise. She picked up the board and threw it across the room. She turned the key to lock her bedroom door and went back to chase the panda with the bucket as though she were trying to trap a giant spider. She managed to catch it and sat on the bucket, staying there a moment clutching the sides, holding her breath every time the bear hit against the plastic and trying hard not to cry.

When her mother called her to dinner, she shouted down that she wasn't feeling good and wanted to go to bed without eating. She picked up the big wooden trunk where she stored her notes and textbooks and put it on top of the bucket, fully immobilizing it. Someone had told her that if you couldn't break the thing, the only way to turn it off was to wait for its battery to run out. So she hugged her pillow and sat on her bed to wait. Trapped under the bucket, the bear went on squealing for hours, banging against the plastic like an overgrown hornet, until, near dawn, the room was left in complete silence.

L i m a

$\bullet\ \bullet$

A TEXT BOX APPEARED on the screen. It demanded a serial number, and Emilia sighed and shifted in her wicker chair. Those kinds of requirements were what most drove her to desperation. At least her son wasn't there, silently timing her as she searched for her glasses so she could reread the instructions. Sitting at the desk in the hallway, she straightened up in the chair to relieve her back pain. She breathed in deeply, exhaled, and, double-checking each number, entered the code on the card. She knew her son didn't have time for any nonsense, and even so she imagined him spying on her from some camera hidden in the corner, suffering in his Hong Kong office at the sight of her inefficiency, just as her husband would have suffered if he were still alive.

After selling the last gift her son had sent her, Emilia had paid the apartment's overdue bills. She didn't understand much about watches or designer handbags or sneakers, but she'd lived long enough to know that anything wrapped in more than two types of cellophane, packaged in felt boxes, and requiring a signature and ID on delivery was worth enough to pay a retiree's debts; it also made it very clear how little a son knew about his mother.

They'd taken her prodigy son from her as soon as the boy turned nineteen, seducing him with obscene salaries and whisking him off to far-flung cities. Now he was never coming back to her, and Emilia still hadn't decided whom to blame.

The screen started blinking again: **Serial number accepted.** Her computer wasn't the latest model, but it was good enough for her. The second message said **Kentuki connection established,** and right away a new program opened. Emilia frowned— what good were these kinds of messages, indecipherable to her? They exasperated her, and they were almost always related to the contraptions her son sent her. Why waste time trying to understand gadgets she would never use again? She wondered this every time. She looked at the clock. It was already almost six. Her boy would surely call to ask what she thought of the gift, so she made one last effort to focus. On the screen the program was now showing a keyboard with controls, like the one on a naval-battle game she used to play on her son's phone, before those people from Hong Kong took him away. Above the keyboard, the program was proposing the action *Wake up*. She selected it. A video took up most of the screen and the control keyboard was summarized at the sides, simplified in little icons. In the video, Emilia saw the kitchen of a house. She wondered if this could be her son's apartment, though it wasn't his style, and the boy would never let the place get so messy or cram it so full of stuff. There were magazines on the table under some beer bottles, mugs, and dirty plates. Farther back, the kitchen opened onto a small living room that was in more or less the same condition.

There was a soft murmuring sound, like a humming, and Emilia leaned closer to the screen to try to understand. Her speakers were old and fuzzy. The sound repeated and she discovered that it was actually a feminine voice: Someone was talking to her in another language and she didn't understand a word. Emilia could follow English—if it was spoken slowly—but this didn't sound anything like English. Then someone appeared on-screen, a girl whose blond hair was wet. The girl spoke again, and the program asked in another text box if it should activate the translator. Emilia accepted, selected *Spanish* for her language, and now when the girl spoke there were subtitles on the screen.

¿Me escuchas? ¿Me ves?

Can you hear me? Can you see me?

Emilia smiled. On her screen she saw the girl come closer. She had blue eyes, a nose ring that didn't suit her at all, and a concentrated expression, as if she, too, had doubts about what was happening.

"Yes," said Emilia, in English.

It was all she had the nerve to say. It's like talking over Skype, she thought. She wondered if her son knew the girl; she prayed this wasn't his girlfriend, because in general, she didn't tend to get along with messy women in low-cut clothes. It wasn't prejudice, just sixty-four years of experience.

"Hola," she said, just to be sure the girl couldn't hear her.

The girl opened a manual the size of her hands, brought it very close to her face, and sat reading for a moment. Maybe she wore glasses, but was embarrassed to put them on in front of the camera. Emilia still didn't understand what this was all about, but she had to admit she was starting to feel a bit curious. The girl read and nodded, stealing an occasional glance at Emilia over the manual. Finally she seemed to make a decision, and she lowered the manual and spoke in her unintelligible language. The translator wrote on the screen:

Close your eyes.

The order surprised Emilia, and she sat up straighter in her chair. She closed her eyes and counted to ten. When she opened them the girl was still looking at her, as though waiting for some kind of reaction. Then she saw on the screen of her controller a new window prompt that helpfully offered the option *Sleep*. Could the program have some way of hearing instructions? Emilia selected the *Sleep* option and the screen went dark. She heard the girl cheer and clap, then speak to her again. The translator wrote:

Open them! Open them!

The controller offered her a new option: *Wake up*. When Emilia selected it, the video came on again. The girl was smiling at the camera. This is dumb, thought Emilia, though she had to admit it was kind of fun. There was something exciting about the interaction, though she still didn't understand exactly what. She selected *Forward* and the camera moved a few centimeters toward the girl, who smiled, amused. Emilia saw her slowly bring her index finger closer, very slowly, until she was almost touching the screen, and then she heard her speak again.

I'm touching your nose.

The subtitle letters were large and yellow, and Emilia could read them comfortably. She activated *Back up* and the girl imitated her, visibly intrigued. It was quite clear that this was her first time as well, and that she was in no way judging Emilia for her lack of knowledge. They were sharing the surprise of a new experience, and Emilia liked that. She backed up again, the camera moved farther away, and the girl clapped her hands.

Wait.

Emilia waited. The girl walked away and Emilia took the opportunity to activate *Left*. The camera turned and she got a better view of how small the apartment was: a sofa and a door to the hallway. The girl spoke again; she wasn't in the frame anymore but the translator still transcribed her words.

This is you.

Emilia turned back to her original position and there was the girl again. She was holding a box at the level of the camera, a few centimeters away. The lid was open and the label on the box said KENTUKI. It took Emilia a few moments to understand what she was seeing. The front of the box was almost all clear cellophane; she could see that it was empty, and on the sides were photos—in profile, head on, and from the back—of a pink-and-white stuffed animal, a pink-and-white rabbit that looked more like a watermelon than a rabbit. It had bulging eyes and two long ears attached to the top. A clip shaped like a bone held them together, keeping them upright for a few centimeters, after which they fell languidly to either side.

"*You're a cute little bunny,*" said the girl. "*Do you like bunnies?*"

Oaxaca

• •

SHE COULD SEE FORESTS and hills just outside the large room they'd been given, and the intense white sunlight didn't remind her at all of the ocher colors of Mendoza. That was good. That was what she had been wanting for a few years now: a new place, or body, or world, whatever it would take for her to change course. Alina looked at the kentuki—that's what it was called on the box and in the user manual. She had placed it on the floor next to the bed, on its charger. The battery's display light was still red and the instructions said that, when first turned on, it had to charge for at least three hours. So, she was waiting. She took a tangerine from the big bowl and wandered around the room while she peeled it, peeking every once in a while through the little window in the kitchen to see if anyone was going in or out of the studios. Sven's was the fifth roof down; she still hadn't gone to see it. She had never gone along with him to one of his artist residencies, so she was measuring her movements, taking care not to bother him or intrude into his space. She had resolved to do whatever was necessary to keep him from regretting the invitation.

He was the one who got the grants, the one who went from here to there with his big monochromatic block prints, "opening art up for the people," "bringing ink to the soul," "an artist with roots." She didn't have a plan for herself, nothing that would sustain or protect her. She didn't have the certainty that came from knowing herself or why she had been put in this world. She was his girlfriend. *La mujer del maestro*—the *maestro*'s lady—as they called her around the Vista Hermosa neighborhood. So if something truly new was happening in her life, even if it sounded like nonsense, the way this weird kentuki did, she had to keep it to herself, at least until she really understood what she was doing. Or until she understood the reason why, ever since she'd arrived in Vista Hermosa, she couldn't stop looking at everything with so much dread, wondering what she could do with her life so the boredom and jealousy wouldn't end up driving her crazy.

She had bought the kentuki in downtown Oaxaca, an hour away from Vista Hermosa, after wandering interminably among market stalls and designer-goods shops full of things she couldn't buy. Yes, she could—she corrected herself every time she caught herself thinking that way: the agreement was that she would keep Sven company on his residencies, and in exchange he would pay for expenses. Still, this was only the first residency, and she had already seen him check the bank account one too many times, combining silences with the occasional sigh.

At the market, she'd walked among stalls selling fruit, spices, and traditional masks, trying not to look at the geese and chickens that were hung by their feet still alive, shaking in silence, exhausted by their own agony. Past the market she'd found a store with glass windows, strangely white and sleek among so many modest street vendors. The automatic doors opened, she went in, and when they closed behind her the noise outside became slightly muffled. Alina was grateful for the air conditioner's gentle purr, and for the fact that all the employees seemed to be too busy attending to other customers or restocking shelves to pay her any mind: she was safe. She took off her scarf, smoothed her hair, and moved along the shelves of shiny household appliances, relieved to be walking among so many things she didn't need. She passed the electric razor section and stopped a few meters farther on. That was when she saw them for the first time, some fifteen or twenty in stacked boxes. They weren't mere toys, that was clear. Several models were out of their boxes so that people could get a better look, though they were high enough that no one could actually reach them. Alina picked up one of the boxes, white and impeccably designed, like the ones Sven's iPhone and iPad had come in, but bigger. They cost $279—a lot of money. They weren't pretty, but even so there was something sophisticated about them that she still couldn't put her finger on. What were they, exactly? She set her bag on the floor and crouched down to get a closer look. The images on the boxes showed different kinds of animals. There were moles, rabbits, crows, pandas, dragons, and owls. But no two were the same, their colors and textures varied, and some of them wore costumes. She looked over more of the boxes, carefully, until she mentally separated five from the bunch. Then she reviewed those five and took two. Now she had to decide, and she wondered what kind of decision she was making. One box said CROW / KRÄHE / 乌鸦 / CUERVO, the other said DRAGON / DRACHE / 龙 / DRAGÓN. The camera on the crow wasn't waterproof. The dragon was waterproof and could produce fire, but she didn't smoke and neither did Sven. She liked the dragon because it looked more sophisticated than the crow, but she thought the crow was more her style. She wasn't sure, though, whether those were the kinds of things she should be taking into consideration for this purchase. She reminded herself that they cost $279, and she took a few steps back. *And yet,* she thought, *I'm still holding the box.* She would buy it anyway, just because, and she'd use Sven's card to do it; she could almost hear him sighing already as he went over the account. She brought the crow to the counter, attentive to the impact of this decision on her mood, and she concluded that the purchase could change some things. She wasn't sure exactly what, or even whether she was buying the right model. The employee who waited on her, barely a teenager, greeted her enthusiastically when he saw her approaching with a kentuki.

"My brother has one of these," he said. "And I'm saving up for one of my own, they're awesome."

Awesome. At that word she started to doubt, not the purchase itself, but having chosen the crow. But then the boy, with a huge grin, took the box from her hands, and the bar code scanner rang out, loud and irreversible. He gave her a coupon for her next purchase and wished her a very nice day.

Once she was back from town and in her room, Alina lay down for a while on the bed, putting her feet on Sven's pillow. The kentuki's box was nearby, still sealed; she wondered if she could return it once it was opened. Then she sat up and placed it on her lap. She pulled off the security seal and opened the packaging. It was a new and expensive object that smelled of technology, plastic, and cotton. And there was something exciting about that, the miraculous distraction of unfurling new cords from their neat coils, pulling the cellophane from two different kinds of adapters, smelling the charger's plastic.

She set everything to one side and took out the kentuki. It was a pretty ugly animal, a big stiff egg covered in gray and black felt. A yellow plastic piece that served as the crow's beak curved down over its stomach, like a necktie in high relief. She had thought the eyes were black, but looking more closely now, she saw that they were simply closed. The creature had three wheels of smooth rubber hidden under its body—one in front and two in back—and the wings, small and close to the body, seemed to have some independence. Maybe they moved or flapped. She fit the animal onto the charger and waited for the contact light to turn on. It flickered every once in a while as if looking for a signal, then went out again. She wondered if she needed to connect it to Wi-Fi, but she checked the manual and confirmed what she thought she'd read on the box: the 4G/LTE was activated automatically, and the only thing for the user to do was place the kentuki on its charger. The purchase included a free year of mobile data, and it wasn't necessary to install or configure anything. Sitting on the bed, she went on reading through the manual for a while.

Finally she found what she was looking for: the first time a kentuki's "keeper" charged the device, they had to have "extreme patience." You had to wait until the kentuki connected to the central server and for the server to link with another user, someone in another part of the world who wanted to be a kentuki "dweller." Depending on the connection speed, the estimated wait for the software to install in both ports was anywhere from fifteen to thirty minutes. It was important not to disconnect the kentuki during that process.

Disappointed, Alina looked over the contents of the box again. She found it odd that, beyond the charger and the manual, there was no other device for controlling the kentuki. She understood that it functioned autonomously, commanded by another user who "dwelled" in the kentuki, but couldn't she even turn it on or off? She scanned the manual's index. She wondered if there were selection parameters for that other user who would inhabit her kentuki, any characteristics that she could personalize or request, and although she looked several times and checked the index, she couldn't find any clues. She closed the manual with an anxious feeling and went to get a tangerine.

She thought about sending a message to Sven, or gathering the courage to visit the studio. She needed to find out how things were going since, a few days before, an assistant had been sent to help with the printing process. The pieces were large and the wet paper was too heavy for just one person. "You can see how it affects the definition of the line," complained Sven, until the gallery owner had the grand idea to get him an assistant. Sooner or later she would have to visit the studio and see just what was being hatched there.

From the bed she looked at the charger's display: the light was green and it had stopped blinking. She sat next to the device with the manual in her hands, reading the rest of the instructions. Every once in a while she looked at the animal, taking in or memorizing details. She had been expecting some kind of latest-generation Japanese technology, one step closer to that household robot she'd been reading about in the magazines of the Sunday paper since she was a kid, but she concluded that there was nothing new: the kentuki was nothing more than a cross between a mobile stuffed animal and a cell phone. It had a camera, a small speaker, and a battery that would last between one and two days, depending on usage. It was an old concept with technology that also sounded old. And yet, the hybrid was ingenious. Alina thought that soon there would be a kind of boom of little animals like this one and that, for once, she would get to be one of those early adopters who listen condescendingly to the enthusiasm of new fans. She would learn a basic trick for it to perform and give Sven a scare as soon as he got back; surely some kind of joke would occur to her.

When the K0005973's connection was finally established, the kentuki moved toward the bed. Alina started in fear and leapt to her feet. The movement was to be expected, but it still surprised her. The kentuki got down from its charging platform, rolled to the middle of the room, and stopped. She crept closer, though keeping a certain distance. She circled it, but the gadget didn't move again. Then she realized its eyes were open. The camera is on, she thought. She touched her jeans—it was a miracle she wasn't just in her underwear, as was usual when she was alone in this room. She thought about turning the thing off until she decided what to do, and then she realized she still didn't know how. Upon closer inspection, she couldn't find a switch on the kentuki or its base. She put it down on the floor again and stood looking at it for a moment. The kentuki looked back at her. Was she really going to talk to it? Like this, alone in the room? She cleared her throat. She moved even closer and knelt down in front of it.

"Hi?" said Alina.

A few seconds went by, and then the kentuki moved toward her. It was silly, yes, but also pretty intriguing.

"Who are you?" Alina asked.

She needed to know what kind of user she'd gotten. What kind of person would choose to "dwell" in a kentuki instead of "keeping" one? She thought that it could be someone who also felt alone, someone like her mother, at the other end of Latin America. Or a dirty old misogynist, or a pervert, or someone who didn't speak Spanish.

"Hi?" asked Alina again.

Apparently, the kentuki couldn't speak. She sat down in front of it and reached for the manual. In the section "First Steps," she looked for a suggestion for this initial exchange. Maybe they recommended questions that could be answered with a yes or no, or maybe there were suggested procedures for beginners, like having the kentuki answer yes by turning to the left and no by turning to the right. Did the kentuki dweller have the same manual she did? Anyway, she found only technical information, advice on care and maintenance.

"Take a step forward if you can hear me," said Alina.

The kentuki moved a few centimeters closer, and she smiled.

"Take a step back when you want to say no."

The kentuki didn't move. This was fun. Suddenly she had a clear idea of what she wanted to ask. She needed to know if the person was a man or a woman, how old they were, where they lived, what they did for a living, what they liked to do for fun. She needed to judge, urgently needed to decide for herself what kind of dweller she'd gotten. The kentuki was there looking at her, maybe as eager to respond as she was to ask.

Then it occurred to her that this crow could peck openly at her private life, would see her whole body, get to know the tone of her voice, her clothes, her schedules; it could move freely about the room and at night it would also see Sven. She, on the other hand, could only ask questions. The kentuki could decide not to answer, or it could lie. It could say it was a Filipina schoolgirl when it was actually an Iranian oil dealer. But she had to show it her entire life, transparently, as available as she'd been to the poor canary she'd had as a teenager that had died watching her, hanging in its cage in the middle of her room. The kentuki chirped and Alina looked at it, frowning. It was a metallic chirp, like the sound a baby eagle would make inside an empty tin can.

"Just a second," she said. "I need to think."

She got up, went to the window that looked out over the studios, and craned her neck to glimpse the roof of Sven's. Maybe desperate from the wait, the kentuki chirped again. Alina heard it move, saw it approach her, tottering at times over the rough wooden floor. When it got close to her, it stopped. They stayed like that, looking at each other.

Then a sound from the studios distracted her and she turned back toward the window. Outside she could see that Sven's new assistant was leaving. The girl was smiling, gesturing toward the studio, maybe toward someone inside who was laughing at her jokes, someone who went on waving at her while she kept looking back to see him as she walked away.

Alina felt some little taps on her feet. The kentuki was

right next to her, its head angled violently upward so it could look at her. She knelt down and picked it up. The creature was heavy; it seemed even heavier than when she'd taken it out of the box. She wondered what would happen if she dropped it. Whether the connection with that particular user would be lost, whether the crow would disconnect, or whether it was built to hold up through a few accidents. The crow blinked its eyes but never looked away from her.

It was charming that it couldn't talk. A good decision on the part of the manufacturers, she thought. A "keeper" doesn't want to know her pet's opinions.

She understood now: it was a trap. Connecting with that other user, finding out who this other person was, also meant saying a lot about oneself. In the long run, the kentuki would always end up knowing more about her than she knew about it, that was true; but she was its *keeper*, and she wouldn't allow the crow to be anything more than a pet. At the end of the day, a pet was all she needed. She wouldn't ask it any questions, and without her questions the kentuki would depend only on her movements, and it would be incapable of communication. It was a necessary cruelty.

She left the crow on the floor, looking back toward where it had come from, and she gave it a little push forward. The kentuki understood: it skirted the legs of the chairs and table, went around the dresser, and moved slowly toward its charger.

Antigua

• •

SITTING ON HIS father's desk chair, Marvin swung his feet, which didn't quite reach the floor. He drew spirals in the margins of his school notes while he waited, and every once in a while he checked the message on his tablet; for more than ten minutes now it had been displaying the words **Establishing connection.** Below that was the warning **This procedure could take some time.** It was information meant for those who had never started up a kentuki before. Marvin, on the other hand, had already witnessed the exciting first connections that two of his friends had made. He knew what steps to follow.

A week before, when his father had discovered Marvin's real grades, he'd made him promise to sit in the study for three hours every day, surrounded by books, doing home-work. Marvin had said, "I swear to God that I will sit for three hours a day at the desk surrounded by books," but he hadn't said anything about studying, so he wasn't really going back on his word. And it would be months before his father caught on that he'd installed a kentuki on the tablet—that is, if his father ever found the time to discover anything else about his son again. Marvin had paid for the kentuki connection using his mother's savings account. It was digital money, the only kind the dead can have. Marvin had already used that account on other occasions, and he was starting to suspect that not even his father knew it existed.

Finally the serial number was accepted. Marvin started in his chair and leaned over the screen. He didn't know how well a kentuki would work from his tablet. His friends who were already kentukis—one in Trinidad and the other in Dubai—used virtual reality headsets; that's what he had learned on, and he was afraid the experience wouldn't be as good on his old tablet. On the screen, the camera came on and everything went white. "Dragon, dragon, dragon," murmured Marvin, his fingers crossed. He wanted to be a dragon, though he knew he had to be open to whatever animal he got. His friends had also wanted to be dragons, but God had known better than they did what each of them really needed: the one who was a rabbit spent his days wandering around the bedroom of a woman who, at night, let him watch while she showered. The one who was a mole spent twelve hours a week in an apartment that looked out over the turquoise waters of the Persian Gulf.

The screen of his tablet was still white, and it took a minute before Marvin realized the problem: the kentuki was facing a wall, and he was too close to focus. He backed up. The application on the tablet was almost as good as the headsets, and still it was hard for him to tell where he was. He turned around and finally saw something: four compact vacuum cleaners lined up one behind the other, almost all the same height as his kentuki. They were shiny and modern; his mother would have loved them. When he moved in the other direction he began to understand: the fourth wall was made of glass and it looked out onto the street. He was in a shop window. It was nighttime, and someone went by outside wearing a hood, so bundled up that Marvin couldn't even guess whether it was a man or a woman, or how old the person was. And then he saw it: snow. It was snowing! Marvin's feet jiggled under the desk. Whatever his friends may have had, none of them had snow. None of them had ever touched snow in their lives, and he could see it now right there in front of him. "One day I'm going to take you to see snow," his mother used to promise him, before Marvin even knew what snow was. "When you touch it, your fingertips will hurt," she'd say, and then she'd threaten to tickle him.

He looked for a way out of the display window. He circled the vacuum cleaners and checked the four corners around him. In the street, a woman stopped for a moment to look at him. Marvin tried to growl, and he managed a soft, sad noise, so deep that, more than a dragon's cry, it sounded like he had a burnt transformer. What animal *was* he? The woman went on with her walk. Marvin tried to push one of the vacuums. It was too heavy, and he could only turn it a little. He moved closer to the glass and spent a while looking for his reflection, but he couldn't get the light in his favor, and so he sat watching the snowflakes fall and turn to liquid as soon as they touched the ground. How much more would it have to snow before it would stick and cover everything in white?

Marvin practiced shortcuts a couple of times on his tablet, making sure he could quickly change from the kentuki controller to Wikipedia if his father came into the room. Then he sat looking at the photo of his mother that hung between his father's old wooden crucifix and a prayer card of the Virgin of Mercy. Maybe God was waiting for the right moment to reveal what kind of animal he would be. He leaned over the screen again. In the display window, he brought the kentuki's forehead up against the glass and sat looking at the empty street. He would find a way out, he thought. At least in this other life, he wouldn't let himself be locked up.

Umbertide

· ·

"PLEASE STOP LOOKING at me like that," said Enzo. "If you don't mind, stop chasing me around the house like a dog."

It had been explained to him that the kentuki was "someone," so he always spoke to it very politely. If it rolled between his legs, Enzo protested, but it was only a game—they were starting to get along. Things hadn't always been like that, though; at first they'd had trouble getting used to each other, and the kentuki's mere presence had been enough to make Enzo uncomfortable. It was a cruel invention: the boy never paid any attention to it, and Enzo had to spend the whole day dodging a stuffed animal rolling around the house. His ex-wife and the boy's psychologist had explained the concept to him together in an "intervention," listing in detail why having one of those gadgets would be good for his son. "It's another step in Luca's integration," his ex-wife had told him. His suggestion of adopting a dog had left them flabbergasted: Luca already had a cat at his mother's house; what he needed now was a kentuki at his father's. "Do we have to explain it all over again?" the psychologist had asked him.

Enzo gathered his gardening tools from the kitchen, then headed out to the backyard. It was four in the afternoon and Umbertide's sky was gray and dark; it would start to rain soon. He heard the mole inside hitting against the kitchen door. It would reach him again before long.

He'd gotten used to the mole's company. He commented on the news to it, and if he sat down to work for a while, he'd lift the thing up onto the table and let it circulate among his papers. The relationship reminded him of the one his father used to have with his dog. Sometimes, just to himself, Enzo repeated some of his father's sayings and mannerisms, the way he would put his hands on his hips after washing the dishes or sweeping the floor and protest affectionately, always with a half smile: "Stop looking at me like that! Stop chasing me around the house!"

But the kentuki's relationship with the boy wasn't working. Luca said he hated how it followed him everywhere, how it went into his room and "messed up his things," how it watched him like an idiot all day long.

Luca had learned that if he managed to let the battery run out, the kentuki's dweller and its keeper would be unlinked, and the apparatus couldn't be used again.

"Don't even think about it," Enzo had threatened him. "Your mother would kill us." But the mere idea of running out the kentuki's battery made the boy's face light up. His favorite game was to lock it in the bathroom or set traps so it couldn't reach its charger. By now Enzo was used to waking up in the middle of the night and seeing the red light blinking on the floor, the kentuki banging against the foot of the bed, begging him to help it find its charger base. The mole always found a way to get his attention. And Enzo (if he didn't want another intervention) had to keep it alive. Because although they shared custody of Luca, his ex-wife had won all of the psychologist's sympathy, so it was best that nothing bad happen to the damned kentuki.

He stirred the dirt and added compost. The greenhouse had belonged to his ex-wife, and it was the last thing they'd fought over before their divorce. Sometimes he remembered that and thought how funny it was that he'd ended up with it. Never before had he noticed how pleasant the dirt in those flower beds was. These days he liked the perfume and the dampness, the idea of a small world that obeyed his decisions with an open, vital silence. It relaxed him, helped him breathe in a little air. And he had bought all kinds of things for it: sprinklers, insecticides, moisture meters, shovels and rakes of every size.

He heard the screen door creak a little. All it took was a slight push to open, and the mole seemed to like that autonomy. It moved quickly to get out of the way of the door's backswing; sometimes it wasn't fast enough, and when the door swung back, it knocked the kentuki over. Then the creature protested, letting out a soft growl, until Enzo went over to help.

This time it landed on its feet, and Enzo waited for the kentuki to approach.

"What are you doing?" he asked. "One of these days I won't be here, and no one else is going to worry about setting you straight."

The kentuki came over and touched his shoes and then backed up a few centimeters.

"What?"

The kentuki looked at him. It had dirt on its right eye, and Enzo knelt down and blew on it.

"How're the basil plants?" Enzo asked.

The kentuki turned and rolled quickly away. Enzo went on adding compost to the dirt, attentive to the little motor as it sped up and left the nursery, and to the bounce the wheels tended to give over the edges of some of the paving stones in the patio. That would grant him a few minutes, he thought. He went to the sink for the scissors and, when he returned, the kentuki was already back, waiting for him.

"So, do they need water?"

The kentuki didn't move or make any noise. Enzo had taught it that, and they had an understanding: no movement meant no, a purring sound meant yes. The quick, short movement forward was an invention of the kentuki's that Enzo still didn't understand. It seemed confused and variable to him. Sometimes it seemed to mean something like "Follow me, please," and other times it could mean "I don't know."

"What about the peperoncini? Did the sprouts from Thursday survive?"

The kentuki moved off again. Its dweller was an old person, or else someone who liked to say they were old. Enzo knew because he asked it questions like a game, and the mole loved to play. He had to engage with it every once in a while, like when you bathe a dog or change the cat's litter. They played their game while Enzo was drinking his beer, lying on the lounge chair in the backyard. It was almost no work at all to think of questions. Sometimes, even, he asked and didn't pay attention to the answer. He'd close his eyes between one sip and another, let sleep catch up to him, and the kentuki had to run into the chair leg to make him keep going.

"Yes, yes . . . I'm thinking," Enzo would say. "Let's see, what does the mole do for a living? Is he a cook?" The mole would stay motionless, which clearly meant no. "Does he grow soybeans? Is he a fencing instructor? Does he own a candle factory?"

It was never very clear what the real answer was, or whether Enzo got it fully right or only close. As the days passed, Enzo found out that whoever it was roaming around his house inside that kentuki had traveled a lot, but so far the places the person had visited were not any of the ones he had named. He also knew that it was an adult man, although it wasn't entirely clear how old. Sometimes he was neither French nor German, and other times he was both, so Enzo thought maybe he was Alsatian. He liked to let the kentuki spin in circles, clamoring desperately for that intermediate option that hung in the air and that Enzo was careful never to pronounce: Alsace.

"Do you like Umbertide?" he'd ask. "Do you like the Italian villages, the sun, the flowered dresses, our women's giant asses?"

Then the kentuki ran around the lounge chair purring at its loudest.

Some afternoons Enzo carried the kentuki to the car and sat it in the rear window so it could look out the back the whole way to Luca's tennis class, then to the supermarket, and back home again.

"Just look at those women," Enzo would say. "Where could a mole come from who's never seen women like these?"

And the mole purred again and again, perhaps out of fury, perhaps out of joy.

Lima

• •

HER COMPUTER HAD also been a gift from her son, several
years back now, wrapped in cellophane and sent from Hong
Kong. Another gift that, at least at first, had brought Emilia
more headaches than happiness. Its bright white plastic had
faded by now, and one might say that they'd gotten used to
each other. Emilia turned the computer on and adjusted her
glasses; the kentuki's controller opened automatically. On the
screen the camera seemed crooked, as if it had fallen. Right
away she recognized the cleavage girl's apartment. Only when
someone picked up the kentuki could Emilia see where she'd
been lying: it was a dog bed. A felt dog bed, fuchsia with
little white polka dots. The girl spoke, and the yellow subtitles
of the translation appeared immediately on the screen.

Good morning.

Her breasts were squeezed into a sky-blue top, and she still
wore the ring in her nose. Emilia had asked her son about his
relationship with this girl, and he'd said he didn't have one.

Then he'd explained over and over how the kentukis worked, and he'd asked her questions about what she had seen and what city she'd been in and how she'd been treated. His curiosity was suspicious; in general, her son wasn't at all interested in his mother's life.

"Are you sure you're a rabbit?" he asked her again.

Emilia remembered something about a "cute little bunny," and she also remembered the box the girl had shown her. She understood—now that someone had taken the trouble to explain it to her—that what she was controlling was a kind of toy shaped like an animal. Were they the animals of the Chinese horoscope? What did it mean, then, to be a rabbit, and not, for example, a snake?

"I love the way you smell."

The girl brought her nose too close to the camera and Emilia's screen went dark for a second.

Whatever could she smell like?

"We're going to do lots of things together. And you know what I saw in the street today?"

She told Emilia a story about something that had happened in front of the supermarket. Though it seemed like a silly thing, Emilia tried to understand; she followed the yellow letters on the screen, but they went by too quickly. The same thing happened to her at the movies: if the subtitles were too long, they disappeared before she could finish reading them.

"And it's a beautiful day," said the girl. *"Look!"*

She lifted the kentuki over her head, facing the window, and for a moment Emilia looked down onto a city: narrow streets, the domes of some churches, water channels, the strong red light of sunset washing over everything. Emilia's eyes opened wide. She was caught off guard—the movement had been unexpected, and the image of that other city awed her. She had never left Peru, never in all her life, if you didn't count the trip to Santo Domingo for her sister's wedding. What city had she seen? She wanted to see it again, wanted the girl to lift her back up. She activated the kentuki's wheels in one direction and the other, turned her head several times as fast as she could.

"You can call me Eva," said the girl.

Eva put her back on the floor and headed toward the kitchen. She opened the refrigerator and a few drawers, and started to cook dinner.

"I hope you like the cushion I bought for you, sweetie."

Emilia left the kentuki facing the girl for a while; she wanted to study the controller carefully. Lift me up again! she thought. Lift me up again! She couldn't figure out how to communicate with Eva. Or was this how it was? In her condition as rabbit, she could only listen? How the hell did you make these animals talk? Now she did have questions, thought Emilia. If she couldn't manage to ask the girl anything, she would call Hong Kong again and ask her son. It was time the boy took a little more responsibility for the things he sent his mother.

A few days later she discovered that she was in Erfurt, or that there was a large possibility that the place her kentuki moved around in was a small German city called Erfurt. There was a calendar of Erfurt hanging on the girl's refrigerator, and then there were the bags that turned up in the apartment and that she left on the floor for days, "ALDI Erfurt," "Meine Apotheke in Erfurt." Emilia had googled it: Erfurt had, as its only tourist attractions, a medieval bridge from the fourteenth century and a monastery where Martin Luther had spent some time. It was at the center of Germany and four hundred kilometers from Munich, the only German city she really would have liked to visit.

For almost a week now, Emilia had spent some two hours a day circulating around Eva's apartment. She'd told her girlfriends about it at their Thursday coffee, after swimming. Gloria asked what was this thing that Emilia called "kentuki," and as soon as she understood she decided to buy one for her own house, for the afternoons when she took care of her grandson. Inés, on the other hand, was horrified. She swore she wouldn't set foot in Gloria's house if she ever bought such a gadget. What Inés wanted to know—and asked several times, hitting her finger against the table—was what kind of regulations the government would implement for a thing like that. You couldn't just count on people's common sense, and having a kentuki running around was the same as handing a stranger the keys to your house.

"Plus, I don't get it," said Inés, finally. "Why don't you find yourself a boyfriend instead of crawling around on some stranger's floor?"

Inés could be graceless when she spoke, and sometimes it was hard for Emilia to forgive her. She spent a while chewing over her anger, thinking about that comment even after she got home, while she rinsed and hung up her swim towel. Without Gloria, she concluded, her friendship with Inés wouldn't last a day.

By the end of the week, Emilia had established a new routine. After washing the dishes she made a little tea and punctually tuned in to Eva's apartment. To Emilia, it seemed the girl was starting to get used to that late but regular hour when she woke the kentuki. Between six and nine at night, German time, Emilia circulated around the girl's legs, attentive to what was happening. On Saturday, in fact, when Emilia roused the kentuki and the girl wasn't there, she found a sign stuck to one of the chair legs, a few inches from the floor. She had to transcribe it on her phone, letter by letter, to understand what it said, and she was pleased when she found that it really was for her:

"*My pet, I am going to the grocery store. Without delay, I return in thirty minutes, easy. Attentively, your Eva.*"

She would have liked to have the original paper with the girl's fine, slanted handwriting to hang on her refrigerator, because in spite of the German and the shiny fuchsia ink, it was a sophisticated hand, something that could have been sent by a distant relative or a friend abroad.

Eva had bought her a dog toy, but since Emilia didn't use it, she usually left some other kind of object close by to see if any of them tempted her. There was a ball of yarn that she sometimes pushed around and a little leather mouse whose functionality Emilia never managed to decipher.

Though she appreciated the good intentions, what she was really interested in was seeing the things the girl had around the apartment. She watched when she put away the groceries in the cupboards, when she opened the cabinet in the hallway or the wardrobe across from the bed. She looked at the dozens of shoes Eva tried on while she got ready to go out. If something caught her attention, Emilia purred around the girl and she would leave it on the floor awhile. Like that foot massager she'd shown her once. You couldn't find anything like that in Lima. It was very disappointing to think that her son kept sending her perfumes and sneakers when he could make her so happy with a foot massager like that one. She also purred to ask Eva to lift her up, or if she wanted to get out of the dog bed.

One afternoon at the Lima supermarket, when she'd gone to buy her coconut cookies and granola and had found the shelf empty, she had also purred in silence, to herself. She was immediately ashamed, wondering how she could go around playing bunny just anywhere. Then one of her neighbors passed the aisle, and the woman looked so old, gray, and crippled as she murmured to herself about her hardships that Emilia recovered a certain amount of dignity. I may be crazy, but at least I'm modern, she thought. She had two lives, and that was much better than barely having one and limping around in free fall. And finally, what did it matter if she made a fool of herself in Erfurt? No one was watching, and it was well worth the affection she got in return.

The girl ate dinner around seven-thirty, while she watched the news. She'd carry her plate to the sofa, open a beer, and lift the kentuki up next to her. It was almost impossible for Emilia to move around on the couch cushions, though she could turn her head and look out the window at the sky, or study Eva from closer up: the texture of her clothes, how she had done her makeup, the rings and bracelets she was wearing. She could even watch the European news. She didn't understand anything—the translator worked only on Eva's voice—but the images were almost always enough for her to be able to form an opinion about what was happening, especially since there weren't many people in Peru following German news. Talking about it with her friends, she realized right away that she had privileged insight, and that people didn't tend to be up-to-date on the latest news from Europe in all its detail.

Every other day, around a quarter to nine, the girl got dressed to go out and left Emilia alone. Before turning out the lights, she'd carry the kentuki over to the dog bed. Emilia knew that once she was there it would be hard to move again, so sometimes she tried to escape before Eva lifted her up, running from side to side and hiding under the table.

"Come on, honey, it's getting late!" Eva would say, and even if she occasionally got mad, she usually laughed while she tried to trap her.

Emilia told this to her son, and the boy was alarmed.

"You mean you spend the whole day running behind her, and when the girl leaves, you stay in the dog bed?"

Emilia was at the supermarket doing the shopping, and her son's tone scared her. She stopped her cart, worried, and adjusted the phone on her ear.

"Am I doing it wrong?"

"It's just, that means you're not charging, Mom!"

She didn't really understand what her son was talking about, but she liked that ever since she'd had the kentuki, he answered right away when she sent him messages with questions and updates, or with stories about Eva. Emilia wondered whether her son had known ahead of time that giving her a kentuki would bring him closer to his mother, or whether the gift was bringing him more problems than he'd bargained for.

"Mom, if you don't charge every day, the battery's going to run out, don't you see?"

No, she didn't see. What was it she had to see?

"If the battery reaches zero, then the link between users is lost, and it's goodbye, Eva!"

"Goodbye, Eva? I can't turn on again?"

"No, Mom. It's called 'planned obsolescence.'"

"Planned obsolescence . . ."

She was at the canned food shelf when she repeated those two words, and the stock clerk looked at her curiously. Her son explained it to her again, speaking louder into the phone, as if Emilia's problem were with her hearing. Finally she understood, and she confessed disconcertedly that she had been controlling the kentuki for a week without charging. He sighed in relief.

"She's charging you," he said. "Thank goodness."

Emilia reflected on this while she was waiting to pay. So that meant that when she went to sleep and left her kentuki in the dog bed until the next day, the girl took her out of it, set her on the charger, and then returned her to the bed once the charge was complete. Emilia shifted the peaches from under the cans of peas and put them on top so they wouldn't get bruised. So every day, someone at the other end of the world did all that for her. She smiled and put her phone away. That was some attention.

Barcelona

· ·

THE MOSSÈN CINTO wasn't just a home for the elderly; it was one of the most beloved and best-equipped institutions in the Vila de Grácia neighborhood of Barcelona. It had five treadmills, two Jacuzzis, and its own EKG machine. Now that all the repairs to the front of the gym had been paid for, Camilo Baygorria wanted the remainder of that year's budget to go toward recreation. It had taken him forty-seven years as administrator of the place to reach these recent months of bonanza, and now he needed something that would make all the difference, something the families would notice immediately when they visited and would talk about for the rest of the week.

It was Eider, the head of nursing, who suggested the kentukis. She thought it would be hard to convince Camilo of her idea, though she knew there was already one in his family: a nephew had bought one with his savings. It never would have occurred to Camilo to buy such a gadget for geriatric patients, but even so he took the risk. He thanked Eider for the idea, and immediately they ordered two rabbit kentukis. Eider herself made a little blue hat with a brim for each of them, with two holes for the ears and the home's logo on the front.

They turned them on together in the main hall after lunch. The K0092466 established a connection after two hours and twenty-seven minutes, and the K0092487 connected after three hours and two minutes. There were already three hundred seventy-eight servers repeating the connections around the world, and even so they were still overloaded: wait times for the initial configuration were growing ever longer.

As soon as the two kentukis started to move, some of the elderly residents came closer. The rabbits circled between their feet and they laboriously raised their legs to let them pass, as if the gadgets were windup toys incapable of dodging obstacles. Not ten minutes had passed when one of the kentukis parked itself in front of the main window and didn't move again. It had disconnected on its own, and Eider had to explain several times to Camilo that there wasn't much they could do about it. As far as she knew, if a kentuki's user wanted to abandon the "game," it couldn't be used again.

"Do you think it's because of the old folks?" asked Camilo.

Eider hadn't thought about that. It had never crossed her mind that now, in addition to all the specifications you had to read if you bought a new appliance, you also had to think about whether you were worthy of having that object live with you or not. Who would ever stand before the store shelves and think about whether the fan she was considering buying would agree to fan an elderly father in diapers while he watches TV?

"Do you think we could lose the other one, too?" Camilo took her by the elbow, frightened.

Eider stood looking at him. For the first time, she saw that Camilo was now as old as the aged people he cared for, and she understood the terror in his question. Near them, an old man picked up the other kentuki to study it. He talked to it with his mouth almost touching its snout, fogging up its eyes. He tried to put it back on the floor but couldn't bend over; he dropped it with a cry of pain, and the kentuki hit the ground and rolled. Eider went over to the rabbit, set it upright again, and followed it as it moved among the tables of the dining hall, making sure the residents left it alone.

"Eider." It was Camilo's voice as he came up behind her.

She was about to turn toward him when she saw an old woman hurrying after the kentuki, and behind her a male nurse who was trying to stop her. Suddenly, with a speed that Eider thought seemed premeditated, the kentuki turned toward the little fishpond that was in the center of the yard and headed off at top speed. What was it doing? Eider's instinct was to run toward it, but Camilo held her back. The rabbit didn't stop, and it toppled into the water. The old woman cried out and waded into the pond, the nurse behind her.

"Eider," said Camilo, pulling again at her elbow. "Are you sure there's no way to recover anything? Not anything?"

Outside, the nurse had managed to sit the old woman on the edge of the pond. She was drenched and crying as she reached out her arms toward the kentuki that, a few feet away, slowly sank under the water.

Oaxaca

• •

SHE KEPT RUNNING every morning. If she went back to Mendoza in two months, at least she could say she was in good shape now. It wasn't the kind of achievement she was looking for, but there wasn't much else to do. Although she *had* found ways to entertain herself. There was the library—it had been a long time since she'd allowed herself the luxury of so much reading—and the kentuki, too. She had to admit the kentuki was interesting.

When Sven saw it for the first time, he stood for a while in front of the crow, while the crow looked up at him from the ground. The two of them studied each other with so much curiosity that Alina had to make an effort not to laugh. Sven was a tall, blond, Danish man; in Mendoza she had to watch over him like he was a fifteen-year-old girl. He was naive and overly friendly, so he got cheated, robbed, mocked. In the galleries of Copenhagen, though, surrounded by peers and always seconded by some energetic little assistant, he seemed to Alina like a prince who was slipping through her fingers. The jealousy she'd been feeling since they'd arrived in Oaxaca was a mere shadow of what it had been a year earlier in Denmark, in the first months of her relationship with Sven. Over time that distress had turned toward something else. Before, it had tormented her, focused her gaze only on him; now, on the other hand, it distracted her. She was losing interest, and jealousy was the only thing that returned her attention to Sven every now and then. There was also another indulgent state she loved, one that was hers alone. She'd lock herself in a room and concentrate on marathon binges of TV series, only to return to reality many hours later. She was left "fragmented"— that's how Alina liked to describe it. It was a dizziness that put her dumbest fears to sleep and, maybe because of the isolation itself, returned her to the world clean and light, open to the simple pleasures of a little food and a good walk.

But sooner or later her path crossed Sven's again, and she remembered that her life was made of things that could always be lost, like his charming smile now as he looked down at the kentuki. Alina had calculated the kind of questions he would ask about the crow and she'd mentally gone over her answers, preparing herself to refute his complaints about its price, its uselessness, the excessive exposure of their private life—although this last factor, she figured, wouldn't be immediately apparent to the *artiste*. He seemed surprised by the little creature, and when he knelt down to look at it up close, he asked a question Alina hadn't considered.

"What should we name it?"

The kentuki turned and looked at her.

"Sanders," said Alina. "Colonel Sanders."

It was a silly name, but it had its charm. She wondered what had made her think the kentuki was male, and at the same time it seemed impossible to imagine that crow with a woman's name.

"Like the old guy from Kentucky Fried Chicken?"

Alina nodded; it was perfect. Sven picked up the kentuki, which protested when they turned it over, looked at the wheels, and studied how its little plastic wings were attached to its body.

"How autonomous is it?"

Alina had no idea.

"Do you think it could follow us to dinner?" asked Sven, and he put it back down on the ground.

It would be fun to try. There was nothing even close to a nice restaurant in Vista Hermosa; in fact, there were no restaurants at all. There were a few women—they'd already been to three—who put out plastic tables in their yards, set them with tablecloths and baskets of tortillas, and offered a fixed menu of two or three dishes. Their husbands were usually eating at one of those tables, always the one closest to the TV, and sometimes they fell asleep with their beer or mezcal in hand. These makeshift restaurants were no more than half a mile away, and Sven figured that, if the technology was like a phone's, the kentuki should be able to follow them with no problem.

Alina, though, was afraid the signal would be lost. She understood that each device held "a single life," but she wasn't clear on whether losing the signal also meant losing the connection.

They went out to the patio and started to walk, and the kentuki followed a few meters behind. Alina listened to its little motor buzzing behind them, aware that, while they stepped so lightly, someone was making a great effort not to lose sight of them. She forgot about the assistant for a moment and felt secure again; she took Sven's hand and he held hers back, loving and distracted. On the asphalt, now out of the residency, the crow had more trouble following them. They heard it turn, slow down, catch up to them again. Then they heard it stop, and they turned around to see what had happened. It was some five meters away, looking off toward the mountains. It was hard to know if it was still there with them, admiring the sunset in the Mexican countryside, or if some technical fatality had suddenly caught up to its soul, and that was all the kentuki they'd have in this life. Alina thought of their $279. Suddenly the kentuki moved; it skirted Sven with a smug air and continued toward Alina.

"And what do you think you're doing?" joked Sven. "Just where are you going with my woman, Colonel?"

They had a good time. They ate chicken with mole and rice, and they left the kentuki on the table through the whole meal. Every time Sven got distracted, the crow pushed his fork off the table and onto the dirt floor. Since it didn't make a noise when it fell, Sven looked for it blindly. He didn't get mad when he discovered the trick. Really, there was absolutely nothing in the ordinary world that could make the *artiste* angry; his energy was channeled toward greater things. Alina envied the calm with which Sven did exactly what he wanted with his life. He moved forward; she bobbed in the wake he left behind, trying not to let him get away. Running, reading, the kentuki—all her plans were contingency plans.

The Colonel dropped the fork again, and Alina burst out laughing. When the kentuki looked at her she winked at him, and he made his crow noise for the first time that night.

"You mess with my woman," Sven said with a laugh, "and you mess with me, too, Colonel." And he bent down again to pick up his fork.

A few days later, when she was leaving the room, she went back at the last moment to get the kentuki. She wanted to show it to Carmen, the residency librarian. Carmen was the closest thing she had to a friend in the whole place. They'd exchange brief, pointed words and discreetly savor the beginning of what would clearly be a great alliance. She tapped on the counter to let Carmen know she was there, left the Colonel beside Carmen's papers, and moved off down the fiction aisle to hide and watch what would happen. Carmen caught sight of the kentuki and went closer. She was wearing all black as always, her wrists covered with studded bracelets. She picked up the crow, turned it over, and studied its base for a while, running her fingers between the wheels. "This one seems like better quality than my two," she said without raising her voice, as if she'd known all along that Alina was watching her.

Alina approached carrying two new books.

"I've never understood," said Carmen, enjoying herself, "what's this little ass for?" And she scratched her painted nails over the USB port hidden behind the back wheels.

Then she set the kentuki on the counter and it moved toward Alina. Carmen said it hadn't even been a month since her ex-husband had given a kentuki to each of her kids, and she had already seen new versions on several occasions.

"My ex says these things grow exponentially: if there are three the first week, there'll be three thousand the second."

"Don't you think it's a little intimidating?" asked Alina.

"Which part?"

Carmen took a step to one side, and behind the kentuki's back she mimed blindfolding her eyes. She pulled her phone from her bag and showed Alina a photo of her two sons with their "pets." They were two yellow cats, and the boys had them in their bike baskets. Each kentuki had a black cloth tied around its head and covering its eyes. That was the only condition Carmen had given her ex-husband: she was afraid the whole thing was a plot so he could have two cameras roaming her house day and night.

Alina stood looking at the picture.

"But why does anyone want to wander around your house with their eyes blindfolded? Where's the fun in that?"

"Right?" said Carmen. "They only have two senses to begin with, and here I go and take one away, and they just keep on toddling around. That's how people are, *manita*, and with a library like this right in town," and she waved her hands at her four empty aisles.

She took the phone from Alina, kissed the image of her sons, and put it back in her bag.

"There was a kentuki that got run over yesterday on the street, right in front of the taxi stand," Carmen went on, as she recorded the books Alina was checking out. "It belonged to a friend of my kids, and the mother had to bury it in the yard, next to the dog graves."

The crow turned toward Carmen, and Alina wondered if Colonel Sanders could understand her.

"Such a shame, now the kid's all broken up." Carmen smiled. It was hard to know what she was really thinking. "And with what those things cost."

"And what was the kentuki supposedly doing alone in the street?" asked Alina.

Carmen looked at her in surprise, maybe because she hadn't thought about that.

"You think it was trying to escape?" she asked, smiling mischievously.

Later, when Alina returned to the room, she set the kentuki on the floor and went into the bathroom. She had to close the door so the crow wouldn't follow her in—he always tried to. She stood by the door until she heard Colonel Sanders roll away. Then she took off her clothes and got into the shower. It was such a good thing she'd never communicated with her kentuki—the more she learned, the more certain she was she'd made the right decision. Without e-mails or messages or agreeing on any other method of communication, her kentuki was nothing but a dumb and boring pet, so much so that sometimes Alina forgot Colonel Sanders was there, and that behind Colonel Sanders was a camera and someone watching.

And so the days passed. Her alarm went off at 6:20 in the morning. None of the artists dared to show their faces around the residency at that hour; the alarm didn't even seem to wake Sven. Alina had time to get up and go down to the kitchen in the common area, have breakfast without any social interaction, and read for a while before she went out to run. Over her second cup of coffee she'd sit straight in her chair, her ass right on the edge, her legs stretched out before her and her feet open in a V. It was her cruising position, and she could read like that for hours. Colonel Sanders went under her legs, pushing the outer points of the V her feet made until he got stuck. Sometimes Alina lowered the book and asked him a question, just to find out if the person controlling him was still there with her, or if he'd left the crow to go do something better. The first option, the idea of someone sitting there and staring at her for hours, always intimidated her, and the second offended her. Wasn't her life interesting enough? Did that whoever-he-was have a life that was so much more important than hers that he'd leave the kentuki hanging until his return? No, she answered herself, if that were true he wouldn't be between her feet now, playing pet at 6:50 in the morning.

"You know what just happened on page 139?"

And Colonel Sanders was almost always there; he'd growl or flutter his wings slightly on either side of his body, but she didn't take the trouble to answer her own questions. At 7:30 she stopped by the room to drop the crow off, and then went out to run in the hills. She turned at the church and moved off the main street. She knew a path that led away from the houses, across fields and down hillocks toward greener areas. She made it farther each time. And each time, she felt stronger. Running didn't make her any more or less intelligent, but the blood flowed through her body in a different way, and her temples pounded. The air changed, and when she got distracted, her brain pumped ideas with incredible speed. When she got back, Sven had already gone down to his studio. Alina took a shower and put on something comfortable, ate her tangerines slowly, faceup on the bed. On the floor, Colonel

Sanders moved restlessly, circling her like a caricature of a bird of prey.

She'd been thinking the day before, thinking too much. And at night, at three in the morning, she'd gotten up and taken a chair to the patio so she could smoke and look out at the hills in the dark. She felt close to some kind of revelation; it was a process that she knew, and the adrenaline of reaching a conclusion made up for the lack of sleep.

And that morning, after coming back from her run and flopping on the bed with her tangerines, she kept turning the matter over and over with the sense she was getting ever closer to an epiphany. She stared at the ceiling and thought that if she were to organize her thoughts to guess what kind of discovery was coming, she would have to remember a piece of information that she hadn't thought about in days: at some point the week before, she'd gone down to the only kiosk in the village, next to the church, and in her distraction she'd caught a glimpse of something she would rather not have seen. Sven's manner of explaining something to a girl. The sweetness with which he was trying to make himself understood, how close they were standing, the way they smiled at each other. Later she learned it was the assistant. She wasn't surprised, nor did it strike her as an important discovery, because a much deeper revelation suddenly caught her attention: nothing mattered. In her body, every impulse asked, *What for?* It wasn't tiredness, or depression, or lack of vitamins. It was a feeling similar to lack of interest, but much more expansive.

Lying in bed, she gathered the tangerine peels into one hand, and the movement brought her to another revelation. If Sven knew all, if the *artiste* was a committed laborer and every second of his time was another step toward an irrevocable destiny, then she was exactly the opposite. The last point at the other end of the continuum of beings on this planet. The *un-artiste*. Nobody, for no one and for nothing, ever. Resistant to any kind of concretion or creation. Her body placed itself in the in-between, protecting her from the risk of ever one day achieving something. She closed her fist and squeezed the peels. They felt like a cool, compact paste. Then she reached her arm over the sheets toward the head of the bed and left the peels in a little pile under Sven's pillow.

Zagreb

· ·

FINALLY GRIGOR HAD a great idea. He called it his "Fallback," and he'd invested the last of his savings in it—his and his father's, if what his father had left could be called savings. He was sure, though, that his Fallback would end his rough patch and put him back in the game. It had been two weeks since he'd had the idea, and he still felt like the work was just getting started. He told his father he'd eat lunch later and then half closed the door to his room. If things went well, soon he could buy the old man a kentuki. It would be good company for him, keep him entertained and maybe even remind him when it was time to take his medicine. Who knew, maybe it would really end up being a big help. He looked at the calendar on the wall above the desk. His severance checks would run out in less than two months, and when his father tried to pay for his yogurt with his bank card and the machine spat it back out, Grigor would be forced to tell him the truth. So the Fallback just had to work.

The tablet's screen told him that the K1969115's connection had found an IP address, and now it was asking for a serial number. The camera turned on and Grigor immediately had to lower the volume. It was a birthday party, and a boy of maybe six years old was shaking him and banging him against the floor. This one won't last long, thought Grigor, though he had already encountered a few surprises. Sometimes the kentukis didn't end up seeing eye to eye with the person they were originally meant for, and someone else in the family adopted them. Like the kentuki that had been connected in Cape Town, South Africa, as the hospital pet of a woman who died a few days later. It ended up traveling with the woman's daughter, stashed in the plane cabin's luggage compartment, to be given to a nephew who lived in the New Zealand countryside. The family set up the kentuki in a shed on their farm on the outskirts of Auckland, where pigs sometimes sat on the charger and Grigor had to hit them on the ass over and over to get them to finally move. That's how fast the luck of a connection could change.

The important thing, Grigor always repeated, was to keep the devices active. It wasn't a technical requirement; that is, even if a kentuki wasn't used in days, the assigned IP connections continued to work—he had studied the matter on social networks, forums, conversations among aficionados, and all kinds of specialized sites, and he was sure that leaving a device unattended didn't mean it would be lost. But if he wanted to sell those connections, he had to keep them alive and on good terms with their keepers. He had to turn them on daily, a good while for each one, and move around and interact. It was a part of the job that he hadn't fully factored in, and it was taking up too much of his time. In fact, he had lost a kentuki for just that reason in the inexperience and disorganization of the first week. He'd neglected it for over two days, and its keeper—a rich and impatient Russian woman who must not ever have had to put up with being ignored for so long—ended up abandoning it. The K1099076, installed on tablet number 3, had given him a red alert with its final message: **Connection ended.**

With that, the connection card of the kentuki's "being" was lost, and so was the kentuki itself. Neither of the two parts could be used again. "One connection per purchase" was the manufacturers' policy—it came written on the side of the box, as if it constituted some kind of selling point. Grigor had seen a boy with the saying printed on his T-shirt some days earlier, when he'd gone out to buy a few more tablets to install more codes. Ultimately, people loved restrictions.

At the birthday party where his eleventh kentuki was fighting for its life, someone finally freed him from the boy's hands and set him on the ground. The paving stones were a porous brick; farther back, between the guests, he caught a glimpse of a large pool. The occasional waiter walked by holding a tray of sodas. A sign said *¡Felicidades!,* which Grigor thought was Spanish. He moved among the guests, and someone followed a little behind him. Every once in a while the person lifted him up, turned him, and set him down with his camera pointing back toward the boy, who in any case wasn't paying him any attention and was entertained enough opening other gifts. *Maybe I'm in Cuba,* thought Grigor. It was something he'd hoped would happen from the very first kentuki he'd connected. If he'd been able to choose a place, he would have picked Havana or some Miramar beach. A dog sniffed at him and fogged up the camera. In his room, Grigor opened his folder and started to fill out a new form. He'd designed the form himself, on day one of Plan Fallback. He'd printed fifty, and he planned to print many more. He wrote down the serial number the program had assigned him, along with the date. He left the boxes for *Kentuki Type* and *City of Kentuki* blank; sometimes it took several days of use to figure those things out. He made his first notes in *General Characteristics*. Upper class, family environment with domestic employees, pool, several cars, possibly rural area, tropical, Spanish language. There was music and the noise of many voices, so the translator was no help at all.

Grigor opened the bottom drawer and counted the cards he had left to activate. Only nine. If Plan Fallback worked out, he felt confident that soon he'd have enough money to buy more connections and more tablets. He had a schedule—eight hours a day—and he had a system—he already administered some seventeen kentukis, which required a certain order. And although he'd decided to raise his prices substantially, the inquiries kept coming in, and he just knew that sales would soon skyrocket. He had let the first three go at very low prices; he'd had to pay his dues, and now the business would start to grow.

His father tapped gently on the door and came in. He was old, but he was still a tall and imposing man. He held a plastic cup in each hand, and he set one on the desk in front of Grigor.

"It's yogurt, son."

He sat on the bed with the other cup. Grigor had tried to explain what he was doing, but his father never really understood. When these new technologies come on the market, he'd told the old man, you have to make the most of the legal lag time before everything is regulated.

"Is this illegal, son?"

For his father's generation, *illegal* was a word that set off alarm bells; for Grigor, it was an overrated term that already sounded antiquated.

"Not until it's regulated," said Grigor.

His cousin had made a fair amount of money using drones to make anonymous deliveries, but that hadn't lasted long. Sooner or later someone with more capital and better contacts showed up. *Regulation* had nothing to do with setting standards; it meant putting rules in place that worked in favor of a few. Companies would soon take over the business opportunity behind the kentukis, and it wouldn't be long before people figured out that if you had the money, rather than paying seventy dollars for a connection card that would turn on in a random corner of the world, it was better to pay eight times that and choose your location. There were people willing to shell out a fortune so they could spend a few hours a day living in poverty, and there were people who paid to be tourists without leaving their houses: to travel through India without a single day of diarrhea, or to witness the arctic winter barefoot and in pajamas. There were also opportunists for whom a connection in a law firm in Doha meant a chance to spend an evening rolling leisurely around over notes and documents that no one should ever get a look at. Then there was that father of the legless boy in Adelaide, who only three days ago had asked him for a "well-behaved keeper" who practiced "extreme sports" in "paradisiacal places." *Money is no object,* his e-mail had said. Sometimes the customers weren't so sure about what they were looking for, and Grigor would send them two or three forms with examples of images and video. Sometimes even he managed to enjoy the connections he maintained. He would wield his gift of ubiquity in secret. He watched his keepers sleep, eat, shower. Some of them restricted him to specific areas, others let him move around with total freedom, and more than once, bored with waiting, he'd entertained himself going through his keepers' things while they were out.

"We save about fifty kunas a week this way, son," said his father, displaying his finished yogurt.

Grigor remembered he was still holding the plastic cup his father had given him. He tried some and understood what his father meant: he wasn't buying yogurt anymore, but had made it himself in the kitchen. Grigor had to force himself not to spit it back into the cup, but to gulp it down with a smile.

Antigua

• •

MARVIN CIRCLED the vacuum cleaners in the shop window, then spent a while looking out at the street. He could tell from the reflection in the glass that the shop was small and dark. It sold appliances. The image in the window didn't quite include him; he still hadn't been able to find a reflection of himself anywhere, and he couldn't answer his friends when they asked what kind of kentuki he was. If he growled, the noise in his tablet's speaker didn't give him any clue, either—it could be the call of a bird of prey just as well as the creak of a door opening. He didn't even know what city he was in, or what his keeper looked like. He'd told his friends about the snow, but they didn't seem too impressed. They'd cracked some jokes about exactly why a princess's ass and an apartment in Dubai were better, then told him that he couldn't even touch the snow, so who cared. Marvin knew they were wrong: if you managed to get out into the snow, and if you pushed your kentuki hard enough against a bank that was nice and white and fluffy, you could leave your mark. And that was just like touching the other end of the world with your own fingertips.

In the shop window, the two square meters he inhabited felt more minuscule every day. He got so bored he'd even tried leaving the kentuki alone and studying instead. After all, the books were right there, so clunky and permanent; sometimes Marvin played a game where he opened them slowly, reverently, like they were relics of an earlier civilization. But he always went back to the kentuki, to that eternal dark night where almost no one ever went by. Once, an older man stopped to look at him and he spun the kentuki in circles, moving from side to side. The man clapped, cheering so loudly that Marvin thought he might be drunk. And another time he saw a boy who was older than him, one who would never have noticed him if they'd gone to the same school. The boy winked at him and kept walking down the street. He passed by again the next day, and the next. Marvin liked that boy and the sound his ring made against the glass every time he knocked on the window to say hi. Did the boy come by just to see him?

One night, after the main lights of the shop window went out, someone picked up the kentuki. For a moment Marvin saw everything: shelves full of radios, blenders, coffee makers, plus a counter and some shining floors. It was a small place, just as he'd suspected, though it was overflowing with plants and merchandise. The person set the kentuki on a table that seemed to be the only one, right in the middle of the shop. Now that he could finally get a look at the whole place, Marvin felt a strange excitement.

He looked around desperately for a mirror, a reflection that would tell him what kind of animal he was. He could finally see the woman who had taken him from the window—she was hefty and old, and she moved diligently from one side of the store to the other, running a cloth over the surfaces around her. She opened a side door to the shop window that Marvin had never seen opened before, and she also took out the vacuum cleaners from the display. As she leaned over the register, for a good while he could see only her legs and the gray feathers of a duster that sometimes peeked out from the other side. On the wall above the counter, seven clocks showed 1:07 in the morning. Marvin wondered why the woman was working at that hour, if she was the store's owner or just took care of cleaning it. He remembered his mother saying that no one can clean up after you better than you yourself, and this woman seemed very committed to her work. He saw her stand up, leave the duster on the table, and pick up the cloth again. Then Marvin tried to put on a show: he spun around on the table opening and closing his little eyes, making his deep, sad caw. The woman turned around to look at him. Marvin shook himself a little on his axis in a way he imagined was like a dog shaking off water, and he rolled over to the edge of the table. He didn't have much more to offer. The woman walked around the table. She came so close that the green apron she wore tied around her waist took up the whole screen. Marvin looked up, wanting to know if she was smiling, and he saw her other hand move above him. He couldn't tell what that hand was doing; the woman's arm had stopped, and hung suspended over the kentuki, connecting them in some strange way. A short, rough sound was repeated through the tablet's speakers, and Marvin finally understood: she was petting him. He gave a brief growl, which he imagined to be like a cat's purr, and he opened and closed his eyes several times, as fast as possible, while the arm's movement made the apron ripple before the screen.

"What a cute little guy," said the woman, in some unintelligible language that the controller translated easily.

Dressed as she was and talking to him so sweetly, she reminded him of the woman who cleaned his own house, this outsize mansion in Antigua full of his mother's curios and ornaments that now no one could bring themselves to get rid of. But that cleaning woman took care of Marvin like he was another orphaned knickknack. The woman in the green apron, however, had touched him. She'd scratched his head with the sincere love of a person petting a puppy, and as soon as she let go of him Marvin spun around and asked for more. Then the woman bent down closer, her immense face filling the screen, and she planted his first kiss on his forehead.

From then on, every other night, the woman took him out of the window and chatted to him while she cleaned. And that's what they were doing one day when she moved the kentuki to clean the table and set him down in front of a mirror. It was only for a second, but at his desk Marvin shouted and flung his arms toward the ceiling, fists closed, as though cheering for a goal.

"I'm a dragon!"

It was what he had always wanted and he repeated it over and over: *I'm a dragon!* sitting at the desk, then standing in front of his mother's photograph, and the next day at every break at school. Things were finally starting to happen at the appliance store.

The woman was usually worked up when she arrived; sometimes she seemed so angry when she spoke that the translator couldn't fully convey her words. But cleaning calmed her down. Maybe it was the only thing that could distract her. Then she would talk to him about her two daughters, and about how badly her husband administered the store. He'd been the one to bring in the kentuki. Her husband was the kind of man who bought everything. When they'd decided to open the business twenty-three years before, she thought it would help him focus, or that at least he'd be entertained by buying things for other people, and he could also enjoy having others buy from him. But the man still managed to acquire an incredible number of useless objects, things that he claimed were essential in order to solve urgent problems that miraculously dissolved immediately after their acquisition.

The kentuki was meant to liven up the shop window—that was how the distributor, the same guy who promoted the line of coffee makers and electric kettles, had sold it to him. He'd delivered the kentuki along with a newspaper article full of statistics about the product, and a promise that, once it was turned on, it would "dance like a monkey" and people wouldn't be able to help stopping in front of the store. What clearly no one had told him was that the little monkey would be connected to a real person, one who might be available only from eleven at night to three in the morning. And who passed the shop window at that hour, other than the town drunks?

Marvin had trouble taking in so much information. So, this woman wasn't his keeper? And if he could only use his kentuki after school—that is, nighttime in this other world—he would never meet his real keeper, the man who had turned him on? And the woman's complaint, that was what bothered him most—would he have to dance like a monkey if he wanted to make them happy? Would it do any good to dance at night? The woman's long droning confused him, but he liked the sweet tone of her voice, her energy as she lectured him, and the noise she made against his casing when she kissed or dusted him.

One night she told him:

"My daughter has one of you at home. And they talk in Morse code. You should learn, so we can chat!"

So Marvin googled the Morse code alphabet and practiced in bed until he fell asleep, growling like his dragon under the sheets. He went over and over the letters of his name.

When the woman said, *"Make a short growl for a dot, a long growl for a line,"* he was ready. He growled his name with utter clarity. The woman said:

"Wait, wait!"

She ran for a pen and paper.

"OKAY! Repeat, little dragon!"

Marvin said his name again in Morse code, and she took notes carefully. Then she cried:

"Marvin! I love it!"

Marvin smiled.

"It's a pleasure, dear Marvin," and he saw her bow as though before a king. *"My name is Lis, at your service."*

That week, Marvin realized that every time the boy who tapped his ring on the window went by, he was writing messages on the glass. He did it in English, which Marvin thought was very cool, even if he left slogans like "Free the kentuki!" or "Slavedrivers!" and the cold conserved the messages on the icy window for too long. He was afraid Lis would see them and think he had something to do with it. He wanted to be

67

set free, yes, the idea wasn't bad at all. But he didn't want to hurt that keeper who wasn't really his keeper, but with whom he had formed a connection anyway.

Sometimes he acted like a monkey, or what he thought acting like a monkey might entail. He spun around in the window, growling and blinking, circling the vacuums and stopping every once in a while in front of one to admire it. It didn't do any good; there was almost never anyone in the street, and at that hour, even if someone passed by and he managed to draw their attention to the lovely casings of those vacuum cleaners, the store was already closed and dark.

"I want to go farther," the dragon growled one night. Lis stopped shaking the duster, took her notebook and her Morse code chart, and a moment later she looked at him and smiled.

"I have two silly daughters," she said, *"and I've waited a lifetime for one of them to say something like that."*

Lis came closer.

"Where do you want to go, little Marvin the Dragon?"

At his father's desk, the question sounded as if she were offering to grant him a wish. Marvin raised his eyes to the books, the old wallpaper, and the portrait of his mother. If he left this house, the portrait would be the only thing he would take with him, though it was too high for him to reach.

"I want to be free," he growled.

"Well, I think that seems like a very good idea," said Lis.

Marvin pictured himself touching the snow. He would have to figure out a way to reach the mountains alone—from the shop window the streets always looked dry, as the snow disappeared as soon as it hit the pavement—but he would find a way. He saw Lis walk away toward the drawer under the shop window and come back with his charger. She left it on the floor with another joking bow, as if making an offering to royalty.

"*Starting now, this whole kingdom shall be yours,*" she said. "*Goodbye, shop window, goodbye, captivity.*"

She picked him up and set him on the floor by her feet.

That wasn't what Marvin wanted. He got onto the charger and surveyed, from his new position, the space that no longer seemed so big or so unknown.

"I want to go outside," he growled.

Lis transcribed his growls in her notebook and then laughed. At his father's desk, Marvin frowned.

"I'll come back."

She looked at him. She was serious as she glanced first at the window, then at the door.

"Please," growled Marvin.

As if she'd suddenly gotten bored with him, Lis left the notepad on the counter and moved off with her duster. She spent a while cleaning. Then she came back, knelt down in front of the dragon, and said:

"*OKAY.*"

And what she said next made Marvin think maybe she, too, had been considering a liberation. Maybe some keepers did for their kentukis what they couldn't do for themselves.

"*I'm going to leave you outside the store: on your charger but under the stairs,*" said Lis. She picked him up and put him beside the cash register. "*You can only go out at night. I want to see you back here every morning so I can put you in the window before he arrives, or else he'll realize. Do we have a deal?*"

The dragon gave a series of growls that spelled out yes. Lis opened the register and took out one of the gift tags they kept in there alongside the money. She showed it to the camera so he could see it—under the logo, in gold letters, were the shop's address and phone number, but the strange letters gave no clue as to where he was. She stuck the tag on his back, just above his rear wheels.

"If anything happens," said Lis as she put him back on the floor, *"look for someone good who can bring you home."*

Before she left him under the stairs, she gave him one last kiss on the forehead.

"Wait!" growled Marvin. He wanted to ask: "What city are we in?"

But Lis must have been thinking of other things, and she walked off without turning around once.

Beijing — Lyon

· ·

CHENG SHI-XU HAD BOUGHT a kentuki card and established a connection with a device in Lyon. Since then, he'd spent over ten hours a day at his computer. His bank account balance was shrinking every day, his friends almost never called anymore, and all the fast food was burning a hole in his stomach. "So this is how you're going to let yourself die?" his mother asked him over the phone, perhaps because she really had been working on her own death for years now, though he was always too busy to notice. For over a month now, though, Cheng Shi-Xu had been focused on something new: he was experiencing the birth of a great love, perhaps the most authentic and inexplicable of his life.

The first thing that happened was that he met his kentuki's keeper. Her name was Cécile and she had received him on her fortieth birthday; he wasn't exactly a birthday present, but Cheng Shi-Xu didn't know that yet. As soon as the K7833962's connection was established, she picked him up and carried him into the bathroom, then held him up in front of the mirror, and then Cheng Shi-Xu could see everything. He was a panda kentuki, covered end to end in fuchsia and turquoise felt. On his belly, in gray plastic letters, were the words *Rappelez-vous toujour. Emmanuel.* Cheng Shi-Xu thought that Cécile was very pretty. Tall and thin, reddish hair, and a face covered with freckles. She smiled at him in the mirror.

"Welcome, my darling," she said.

Cheng Shi-Xu understood a fair amount of French, so he went to the controller's settings and deactivated the translator.

Soon he discovered that the rest of the apartment was just as large and sophisticated as the bathroom, and that it was a kingdom Cécile had generously arranged so her kentuki could have total autonomy. She had placed mirrors at floor level, made small openings—the kind often installed for pets—in the doors and windows that led out to the balcony, and installed a long ramp, hidden behind the three-person sofa, that went from end to end at the height of its broad leather armrests; Cheng Shi-Xu learned to navigate it easily.

Cécile imposed her rules from the very first day without an ounce of shyness, counting out each law on her fingers.

"You can never come into my room. If I come home with a man, you don't leave your charger. If I'm sleeping, or sitting at that desk, it's forbidden to move around the house."

He obeyed.

Outside of those rules, Cécile was attentive and fun. Sometimes they went out on the balcony and she picked him up to show him Lyon. She pointed out the plaza where the world's first black flag of anarchy had been hoisted, and the old storefront where her family's silk shop had once been, and she told him other stories of bombings and revolutions that her grandfather had once told her while standing on that very same balcony.

Cécile and her apartment were a perfect world, and even so, the best of all was in the apartment facing them, the great kingdom of Jean-Claude, his kentuki-keeper's brother. Sometimes they went over to have tea together. Cécile would prepare it, but they would drink it in Jean-Claude's living room while he played the piano.

It was in that apartment where Cheng Shi-Xu met the woman of his dreams.

The first time he saw that living room, he immediately noticed that the glass doors had the same openings as Cécile's apartment. Jean-Claude's own panda kentuki was waiting a little farther in, beside a large orchid's flowerpot. He was surprised to see that stamped on its belly were the same words as on his own: *Rappelez-vous toujour. Emmanuel.* Her name was Titina—or that's what Jean-Claude called her—and she had only one responsibility, which she fulfilled reluctantly. After playing the piano, her master—who was always barefoot—sat down on one of the armchairs across from Cécile to chat and drink tea, and he stretched his legs out in front of him. Then Titina had to rub his feet with her plush body, brushing against them slowly from side to side. Cécile watched them and laughed. If Jean-Claude lost interest, Titina quickly moved away from him toward some other corner of the house. Cheng Shi-Xu followed her like a shadow.

Over time they had managed to communicate. Jean-Claude had painted an alphabet on the bathroom floor, and Titina glided over it with grace. It was a dance that looked lovely when she did it, but that, when it was Cheng Shi-Xu's turn, he performed awkwardly. She wrote in French, he wrote in English. They understood each other perfectly.

"my-name-is-kong-taolin," wrote Titina. "i-live-in-da-an-in-taipei."

Cheng Shi-Xu also told her his name and home. Then he spelled out:

"letters-on-belly . . . ?!"

"emmanuel-bought-1-kentuki-for-each-child-to-receive-after-he-died."

Titina told him more family stories. When Cécile and Jean-Claude were little, their father used to buy them guinea pigs, but the animals barely lasted a year living in their cages. Emmanuel knew that his children were grown and soon he wouldn't be with them anymore. He wanted to give them, at the end, a pet that would last them their whole lives.

The echo of the kentukis' little motors dancing over the tiles were still resonating in Cheng Shi-Xu's head hours later when he fell asleep in his Beijing apartment, thinking over the things they'd said. The next day he googled *Kong Taolin*. The first character was the same as in "Confucius," and although Chen Shi-Xu didn't really know what that augured, he was sure it could only be a good sign. There were dozens of Kong Taolins in Taipei, but only one of them seemed to live in the Da'an neighborhood. She was chubby and had a beautiful smile. He printed the photo and taped it up beside his screen.

Soon Titina gave him her e-mail address. She spelled out the first part of her address on the keyboard of the bathroom, and spent a good while going around in circles, struggling with the obvious fact that there was no @ sign she could point to. Finally she continued her phrase with an *at*, though it wasn't until she added the *.com* that Cheng Shi-Xu realized what it was all about. He jotted it down in Beijing, and in Lyon he danced awhile on the alphabet until he managed to write his own. As soon as teatime was over and he and Cécile went back to her apartment, he opened his e-mail and wrote to Kong Taolin. He signed off with a confession: *"I hate that you have to scratch his feet."* She answered: *"I hate it, too, but in exchange he's teaching me French, two hours every day. I'm learning fast. I'm going to take a test, and once I have my certificate, I'll move to France to work and leave my husband."* So she was married. The news was a blow for Cheng Shi-Xu, though he was grateful for her honesty. She wrote him again: *"I love it when you visit. That's what I do all day long: wait for you to ring the bell."*

He thought that he could help her with her French, too, since he understood Cécile perfectly, but he didn't mention that. She told him she sang for commercials, and she sent a video of a gum advertisement. There was no image of her, but her voice trilled at the beginning and end, and he thought it was sweet and brilliant, a voice even softer than the one he'd imagined for her.

Cheng Shi-Xu searched for Cécile's building on the map. It was easy because he remembered the reference to the plaza and the first black flag, and the place where the family's old silk goods shop had been. It didn't take long to add things up, and he jotted down the address on a piece of paper. He wanted to send Taolin a bouquet of flowers. He thought he would need the siblings' last name, and that it shouldn't be difficult to find, although a second later he imagined Jean-Claude's astonishment when he received the flowers. He could add a card that said *For Titina*, but why send flowers to a kentuki who couldn't hold or smell them? And Jean-Claude wasn't like his Cécile; he wouldn't bother to put them in a vase and leave them on the floor where she could see them. He had to come up with some other kind of gift. What if he kept his plan for flowers, but sent them to her in Da'an? The idea made him sit up straighter in his chair; he googled her again to try to find her exact address. No luck. He woke up his kentuki in Lyon—in the afternoon he usually had it sleep for a while on the sofa's armrest—took the ramp down to the floor, and looked for Cécile. He purred softly a couple of times, and she knelt down and patted his head.

"What's up, big boy?"

That's what she called him.

Cheng Shi-Xu didn't like Jean-Claude, but how he longed for that keyboard he'd drawn in the bathroom for Taolin. Why didn't Cécile do something like that for him? Didn't she want them to talk? He purred a couple more times, aware that his sounds were useless. Finally he tired of trying, turned around, and rolled away.

They started to write each other several times a day. Taolin told him a lot about her father, whom she missed intensely. He'd been good to her, even while he'd also been a dark official in the Cultural Revolution; he'd done things she had never been able to understand. Compared with those stories, Cheng Shi-Xu's family past wasn't so interesting, but Taolin seemed delighted to hear the most ordinary details of his life, like how one summer Cheng Shi-Xu went with his mother and aunt to the National Art Museum. So he sent her an e-mail with photos from the trip, including shots of his mother and aunt. She spent several e-mails analyzing them, until she finally seemed to gather the courage to ask him whether, among all those photos, there wasn't one of him.

Cheng Shi-Xu almost didn't sleep that night, thinking about whether or not to show her his picture. All he knew was that, at almost forty years old, he still hadn't been able to figure out whether he was a handsome man or not. He sent pictures; she didn't answer. The next day, at teatime and after the foot rub, Titina fled to the bathroom, and he followed. She moved quickly over the keyboard.

"yo-lok-like-my-dad," wrote Titina, and she winked an eye.

"lets-talk-on-skype," he said.

She agreed. But that night, in Beijing, Cheng Shi-Xu waited in front of the computer until past two in the morning, and Taolin never appeared. The next day there was an e-mail from her waiting, and when he opened it he read:

"If you write my wife again, I'll send someone to break your face in."

He sat looking at the message; he couldn't remember ever receiving anything so violent in all his life. He didn't know whether to answer or not, whether he should be worried about Taolin, or if she even knew about the message. In Lyon he went down his ramp and into Cécile's room. He was breaking all the rules when he tried to wake her up—she'd gone to bed hours earlier. But he was insistent, banging his kentuki against the legs of the bed. Cécile shifted under the sheets, annoyed, and she threw a pillow at him that left him wheels up. Some seven hours later, in Lyon's morning, Cécile finally picked him up and carried him to the table in the kitchen. She tried to talk to him while she made coffee.

"What's wrong with you, big boy?" she asked. "Do I have to punish you like a dog? What the hell happened to you last night?"

She asked question after question and didn't seem interested in any kind of response. Cheng Shi-Xu moved desperately over the table, trying to say: We have to go to Jean-Claude's! I need his keyboard! Something very bad might have happened to Taolin!

It was afternoon by the time they finally went over. When he entered Jean-Claude's apartment at Cécile's heels, he saw Titina move away from him instead of coming closer, as usual. He realized that seeing this was even more painful than the message he'd received, and even so, he needed to know if she was all right. He rallied, and waited patiently beside Cécile. The siblings talked for a good while, Jean-Claude played an endless piano piece, and then he stretched out his legs and called to Titina, who came shyly over. When the whole foot-rub ordeal was over, Cheng Shi-Xu tried to head to the bathroom with Titina, but she didn't follow him. He came back and tried to push her. They struggled until Titina screeched, and Jean-Claude was beside them in a single bound; furious, he picked her up from the floor. He turned back to his sister, asking for explanations. He didn't hold Titina with affection, not even like an animal, but instead stuck her under his armpit like he was hauling home a watermelon from the market.

"I want that thing out of my house," he said, pointing to his sister's kentuki.

For the next week, Cécile went to tea at Jean Claude's alone. Cheng Shi-Xu was left behind, squeaking and banging against the door, disconsolate. A neighbor would occasionally come out of her apartment and knock on Cécile's door. Then Cheng Shi-Xu was quiet for a while and tried to hold out as long as he could, until his indignation grew again.

Then the most horrible thing Cheng Shi-Xu had experienced in his entire life happened. Something so unfair and inexplicable that he couldn't talk about it, not even to his mother, who still hadn't managed to die and would have greatly enjoyed hearing a good story of someone else's misfortune. One night—an evening when Cécile had gone out— Jean-Claude came into his sister's apartment using his own key. He turned on the lights and looked all around, searching for the kentuki. His eyes were hawklike, his movements more aggressive than ever, and instead of squeaking toward him and pleading for the bathroom keyboard, Cheng Shi-Xu's instinct was to take cover. He slunk behind the sofa. There were better hiding places, but he was afraid that if he moved any more, the sound of his motor would give him away.

Jean-Claude looked for him in the living room, calling to him, and it wasn't long before he found the kentuki. His greeting was suspiciously friendly as he sat down across from Cheng Shi-Xu, on the other sofa. His right hand held a bag, which he set down to one side.

"I was chatting a bit with the lady's husband," he said, "and we've come to an agreement."

Cheng Shi-Xu wondered if he was talking about Taolin's husband—but why would Jean-Claude be in communication with that man?

"All right, Don Juan, are you following me?" All he could

do was listen, so he rolled closer. "This is what we're going to do: Taolin needs to focus on her French classes, and I need for people I don't like to stop trespassing in my home."

It was the first time he'd heard her name from Jean-Claude's mouth—he always called her Titina. Hearing "Taolin," from Jean-Claude made Cheng Shi-Xu think maybe the two of them also wrote to each other.

Jean-Claude reached into his pocket for something. He pulled out a screwdriver and knelt down before the kentuki to show it to him with a conceited elegance.

"I bet you can't guess who sent this from Da'an?" he said.

He left the screwdriver on the floor and took a white box from the bag. It took Cheng Shi-Xu a moment to recognize it. In fact, he didn't understand what was going on until Jean-Claude opened the box and pulled out a kentuki.

"But we can't let Cécile feel sad, now can we?" he said.

The kentuki in the bag was identical to Cheng Shi-Xu's, the same fuchsia and turquoise felt panda, the same belly with the same gray plastic lettering: *Rappelez-vous toujour. Emmanuel.* Although Cheng Shi-Xu tried to get away as fast as he could, Jean-Claude didn't have to make any effort at all to catch him. On his screen in Beijing, the Lyon living room shook violently, and in the speakers, his own squeaks sounded hysterical and metallic. As Jean-Claude struggled with the screwdriver to open the kentuki's base, Cheng Shi-Xu moved his wheels from one side to the other, but he knew there was nothing he could do. He heard the sound of plastic giving way, and then Jean-Claude's stilted voice saying, before he definitively pulled out the battery:

"Now we'll love you more than ever, Don Juan."

A second later, the controller on his computer closed and a red warning announced, **Connection ended**, followed by the K7833962's total connection time: forty-six days, five hours, thirty-four minutes.

Umbertide

• •

ENZO WAS LOOKING over the greenhouse plants while he finished his coffee. The basil was smooth and shiny; he pulled off a leaf and smelled it. It was strange to be checking on the plants without the kentuki rolling around under his feet. They had spent a good weekend together, but Sunday afternoon something had gone wrong, something Enzo still didn't understand, and since then the mole hadn't shown its face. He called to it while he watered the last spices. He called it "Mole" or "Kentu" or, most often, "Mister." He went back to the house and checked under the table and in front of the sliding glass door where the kentuki sometimes sat watching the neighbors go by. He also looked for it next to the armchair's leg, a corner it was hard for Enzo to get to, and where the kentuki usually went when it wanted someone to turn the TV to the RAI channel.

"You want to practice some Italian, Mister?" Enzo would ask if he saw it there.

He'd turn on the TV and flip through channels, looking for the kentuki's program. When finally the tits, asses, and shouting matches appeared, the kentuki purred, and Enzo would smile at the sound.

Luca came to kiss him goodbye, then left with his 7:40 a.m. slam of the door. When his mother honked the horn outside, the boy had two minutes to gulp down the last of his milk, put on his sneakers and backpack, kiss his father, and leave. If he took any longer, they heard the doorbell instead of the horn, and that wasn't good for anyone.

Enzo called to the kentuki again. It wasn't in the dining room or in any of the bedrooms. He was afraid his son had trapped it somewhere again to keep it away from its charger. He went back through the kitchen and out to the garden. The kentuki wasn't anywhere.

The day before, he'd taken Mister out to see the historical downtown. Instead of putting him in the back window ledge of the car, he'd set him on the passenger seat on a stack of cushions. He buckled the seat belt and cleaned the mole's eyes with the cloth he used for the windshield, to be sure Mister's sight was perfectly clear. As they drove, he pointed out the Torre della Rocca and the Collegiata di Santa Maria della Reggia. Then they took a slow turn around the canal and the small farmer's market that was held the first weekend of every month. He figured any foreigner would enjoy seeing the sights of a city as small and beautiful as his. Finally he parked around the corner from the Piazza Giacomo Matteotti; he wanted to stop by the pharmacy to say hi to his friend Carlo. He carried the mole under his left arm, against his chest, the way he sometimes carried his groceries.

"I can't believe it," said Carlo when he saw Enzo come in. And Enzo had to explain that the kentuki was his son's, and then go into the whole matter of his ex-wife and the psychologist. He left Mister on the counter so he could wander freely, while Carlo's eyes followed him closely.

"And where are those people today?" asked Carlo. "Why is it always the man of the house who ends up walking the dog?"

"Those people" disappeared most Thursdays through Sundays, thought Enzo, when the boy usually went to his mother's house and he was left alone with the kentuki. He smiled and said nothing. They shared a beer—Carlo always kept a can in one of the pharmacy's refrigerators—as they chatted a while longer.

Back in the car, Enzo saw an old woman crossing the square with another kentuki. She had it on the ground behind her, attached to a leash. Every once in a while she stopped to wait for it, scolding it and tugging impatiently on the leash. He had already seen one or two kentukis in Umbertide, at Luca's school and at the bank counter, but for the first time he realized that, for someone who didn't know those gadgets contained an actual human being, people with kentukis could seem very strange, even crazier than folks who talked to pets or plants. He got into the car with Mister, and the two of them sat watching the old woman and her kentuki, who were now each pulling at the leash in opposite directions.

Back home, he organized and cleaned up the kitchen, picked up Luca's things that were scattered around the living room, and carried them to his bedroom. The boy's room was a disaster. Enzo didn't like to pressure him about tidiness—it had never worked on him when his own mother hounded him ceaselessly about it, so why would it work on his son? Sometimes Mister would help by pushing a stray sock from the kitchen to the bedroom, or else he'd patiently, one by one, collect the candy wrappers the boy left all over the house, piling them in places where it would be easier for Enzo to pick them up. Enzo would watch, curious at such displays of devotion. If Luca was home, Mister followed him everywhere, though he kept his distance, careful not to bother the boy. He didn't hit against Luca's legs or try to catch his attention like he did with Enzo, wanting him to ask questions or tell him where the charger was. Maybe because he knew that if he got within reach, the boy would catch him, lock him up somewhere, or, as was becoming his habit, put him on a shelf where he couldn't get down until Enzo rescued him. But Mister was a faithful guardian, and he allowed himself only occasional moments of leisure—with the RAI or at a window—when the boy was out of the house. If Enzo ordered Luca to do his homework and the boy got distracted, the kentuki came to Enzo to let him know. If the boy fell asleep watching TV, the kentuki came to Enzo, and he could guess what it was about— he'd pick Luca up and carry him to bed.

Mister had perfectly assimilated into his role as co-parent, and Enzo felt grateful. Rich or poor, in his other life the kentuki was, clearly, someone with a lot of free time. What kind of life did Mister have on the other side? There didn't seem to be anything that would take him away from his existence with Enzo and Luca. He was there from morning to night. There were a few times when Enzo found him on the charger during the day, but that happened only when the boy had made sure he couldn't charge during the night. They'd been together for two months now. Every once in a while, when he saw the kentuki holding the screen door open so he could take the garbage out, or when at nighttime it went back and forth from Enzo's bedroom to the hallway to indicate he'd forgotten to turn off the outside light again, Enzo stood looking at the little creature with a mixture of pity and gratitude. He knew that the animal wasn't really a pet, and he wondered what kind of a person could have such a need to take care of them, to nurture—a widower, maybe, or a retiree without much to do. But above all, he wondered whether there wasn't something he could do to repay such attention.

And so, the day before, back home after the tour of Umbertide, he opened a beer and went to sit on his lounge chair in the garden. Mister whirred around him, and Enzo leaned over so he could see the kentuki. He called it over. He waited until the mole was right in front of him, and then he ventured to ask:

"What are you doing here all day with us?"

They were still for a moment, looking each other in the eyes. Enzo took a long sip of his beer.

"Why do you do this, Mister? What do you get in return?"

There were several questions, and none of them could be answered with a yes or a no. Enzo understood how frustrating it was for both parties, but still, what more could he do? This is bullshit, thought Enzo, I'm getting sentimental about a pile of felt and plastic. The kentuki didn't move, or purr, or blink. Then Enzo had an idea. He left the beer on the ground and got up from his chair. Maybe alarmed by the sudden move, the kentuki looked up and kept him in view. Enzo went into the house and returned a moment later with a pen and paper.

"Mister," he said then, as he sat back down in front of the kentuki and wrote his phone number. "Call me." He held the paper in front of the kentuki. "Call me now and tell me what I can do for you."

He knew he was proposing something a little strange. It crossed a line, as if he were using his son's toy for his own benefit—something that his ex-wife and the psychologist would definitely not approve of—and at the same time, he couldn't believe that this genius idea hadn't occurred to him sooner.

When he thought that enough time had passed for anyone to write the number down, he left the paper beside the beer and went to get his phone. When he came back, the kentuki was still in the same position. Maybe, in his own house, Mister still had a landline and was walking toward it as fast as he could, as excited as Enzo was as he waited for the call. He thought it was lucky the boy wasn't there, and he wondered if it would be a good idea to tell him later about this phone call they were about to have. The kentuki was still motionless before him. Maybe the old man behind it had his hands full looking for something to write with and couldn't also manage the device. Enzo waited a while longer still, waiting for the phone to ring out in the silence, unable to keep from smiling. He waited five minutes, fifteen, an hour, but the phone never rang. Finally he got up and went to get another beer. He came outside again and was so enraged to find the kentuki in the exact same position that he went right back in and started to make dinner. At some point he heard Mister struggle with the screen door and then whir across the living room. Enzo turned toward the hallway and saw him move off toward Luca's room.

"Hey!" He wiped his hands on a towel, starting to go after him. "Pssst. Mister."

The kentuki didn't turn back toward him, didn't stop, and Enzo was left alone in the living room trying to understand what the hell was going on with the mole.

After that, the kentuki completely disappeared from sight. The next day, sick of looking for him, Enzo went out to check the garden and the nursery, clucking his tongue and whistling. Sometimes, when he called the kentuki, Mister would make his purring sound. They'd do it two or three times, and that's how they would find each other. But this time there was no trace, and somehow that confirmed his suspicion that the matter of the call had disturbed Mister.

He found the kentuki a few hours later, by chance. It was in the little coat room, inside a closet that, apparently, Luca had locked. Mister had used up almost all his battery trying to get out of the dirty-clothes basket—an absolutely impossible feat for a kentuki. He was agonizing with a spent purring noise, such a weak lament that Enzo could hear it only if he held Mister very close to his ear.

Lima — Erfurt

· ·

EMILIA WOKE HER KENTUKI and found the camera view sideways. On Eva's kitchen floor, she could see four bare feet that came and went. Four bare feet? Emilia frowned and looked around for her phone. Though she wasn't about to call her son over that kind of nonsense, the situation was nevertheless alarming, and it was good to know the phone was handy. She recognized Eva's feet and she understood that the others—heftier, hairier—belonged to a man. She tried to move the kentuki, but someone had laid her down on the dog bed. She squeaked. It wasn't something she did often, so it worked. Eva walked over to her and put her on the floor, righting the camera. That clarified many things, and also confirmed Emilia's fears: Eva was naked. The man who was with her was also naked, and now he was making something on the stove, brandishing a frying pan. Eva blew a kiss at the camera and walked toward the bathroom. For a moment, Emilia hesitated. Normally, she would follow; Eva never closed the door and Emilia would wait for her outside, the kentuki's back discreetly against the hallway wall. But now there was a man in the house.

Wasn't it dangerous to leave that stranger alone in the kitchen? Would Eva expect her bunny to watch over what was happening while she was in the bathroom? She stayed in the hallway threshold, looking toward the kitchen. The man opened the fridge, took out three eggs, broke them into the pan and left the shells on the counter. The garbage can was just inches away, though maybe the man didn't know that. He shook the pan with a slight inclination of his head, as if following some kind of technique, and he belched. It was a dry, soft sound that most likely Eva didn't hear from the bathroom. Then he opened the fridge again and made a noise. Emilia thought he must be speaking German, but it was impossible to know because the translator didn't seem to work with him. Then the man turned toward the living room. His dark, hairy penis hung down between his legs—and where else would it hang? She gave a start in her wicker chair and then laughed to herself. She'd almost forgotten what one looked like by now. She needed to go to the bathroom, too, urgently, but she didn't want to leave Eva alone with that man; she couldn't go now. Nor could she move the kentuki: she couldn't tell whether the man was looking toward the living room or at her, and although she wanted to hide, she knew any movement might give her away. She risked it anyway. She sat back down in her seat and moved the kentuki a few inches. She realized her mistake when the man's eyes followed her. He walked toward her, and Emilia turned the kentuki and withdrew as fast as possible down the hallway toward the bathroom. She heard steps behind her. She tried to speed up, pressed her finger so hard on the button it hurt, but she couldn't go any faster. The man's steps sounded very close, and Emilia stopped breathing.

She almost made it to the bathroom door, but before she could glimpse Eva, she was lifted from the floor. She squeaked. She saw a skylight in the hallway ceiling that she'd never known was there, and then his face, enormous on the screen, a couple days' worth of beard and his eyes too blue, too big, before her. There was something crazy about them, and they were looking right at her. Now it was just one eye, as if a giant had picked up her house and had found a hole in her computer screen through which to peer in at her. He'd found her. He said something that sounded like a curse word and that the translator didn't clarify. Emilia let go of the mouse and drew her nightshirt closed with both hands. Then she heard a sound that made her despair even more: the shower. Eva had turned the shower on. Her little girl who lived alone and apparently without any adults nearby had brought a man home and left him alone while she showered. In her house, Emilia stood up again. She was furious, and she couldn't leave the computer. The kentuki swung in the air—they were returning to the living room.

The man set the kentuki on the table and leaned over to look at it. When he straightened, his member took up Emilia's entire screen. It didn't look at all like her husband's—his had been so much softer and paler. The man talked to her in German while his manhood stared at her. Maybe all male genitals spoke only German, and that's why she and her Osvaldo had never understood each other well. She let herself smile, a little proud of how modern she suddenly felt, controlling her kentuki while she gracefully rose above the memories of her greatest communication failure, attentive to that large sex of a German male that now she could look at without feeling shame. It was a story worth telling on Tuesday to the girls after swimming; she even thought about taking a picture. Then she turned around on her keeper's table and saw something she couldn't laugh at. The man was digging around in Eva's purse. He took out her wallet and opened it, looked at the documents and cards, counted the money and took out several bills. Emilia squeaked—how frustrating that that was all she could do. He moved to pick her up, but she got away. She tried to spin in circles, squeaking like a true chicken as he tried to catch her. She managed only a few seconds of agility, until finally he was able to pick her up again and carry her into the kitchen. The camera's movement made her dizzy. When it stopped, she realized that the German was about to put her under the faucet. For a moment she saw the eggshells from very close up, the slime of the egg white spreading over the clean counter. The faucet spat out a great stream of water. If she got wet, she thought, something inside her could break, malfunction. She squeaked again. She heard the hollow sound of the water hitting her head. She squeaked once more. Could that brutish hunk of meat really do away with her? She shook her body as hard as she could and managed to slip from his hands and fall into the sink, where he caught her again.

"Are there any eggs for me?"

Eva's voice interrupted, soft and fresh, as the man's hand again imprisoned Emilia's kentuki. He seemed to be explaining himself, and Eva listened distractedly as she dried her wet hair with a towel. Then she reassured him there was no need to clean the kentuki, she got it dirty herself sometimes, the only important thing was to keep the eyes spotless.

"Because that's where the camera is," said Eva, taking her bunny from him.

Emilia repeated to herself what Eva had just said. When she said "the camera," the girl was referring to her, to Emilia, for the first time. And that meant taking for granted that there was someone inside the bunny, someone Eva loved and took care of. This happy revelation was even more intense for her than the German's private parts. What a day, thought Emilia. Eva put her back down on the floor and walked away. She was still naked from the waist down, and Emilia felt that she loved that little girl more than ever. They were important to each other; what they experienced together was real. She followed Eva to the living room, followed her naked little ass, small and perfect, which filled her with the kind of tenderness she'd felt so many times for her son, when he was still a boy. Eva flopped onto the sofa and Emilia softly tapped against her toes. She managed to get the girl to pick her up and set her beside her, looking toward the kitchen. The man came over with the food served on a plate. He asked a question—maybe whether he should bring salt and pepper, because he headed back to the kitchen, still talking. Emilia couldn't understand him, she only intuited his words from Eva's response: *"Yes,"* said the girl, *"of course there's someone there, inside the bunny."* And the man in the kitchen stopped smiling and looked Emilia in the eyes.

Antigua

· ·

MARVIN CLOSED THE OFFICE DOOR, turned on his tablet, and propped it on top of his books. He no longer made sure to always have his notebook open and pen in hand just in case his father came in and he had to switch quickly from screen to books. The whole time he'd been serving his sentence of three hours a day in that room, not once had his father or the housekeeper bothered to check on him. At dinner, his father would ask how things were going, whether he was getting good grades. His report card would come in three weeks and it would be terrible, but that didn't matter: Marvin was no longer a boy with a dragon; he was a dragon with a boy inside him. His grades were a minor concern.

His keeper was true to her word and set him on his charger at the foot of the stairs. Marvin watched her walk away and waited a bit before moving. Then he rolled down from the charger and guided his dragon the length of the gallery, finally peeking out onto the sidewalk. There was no one in the street. Not a single snowflake. He rolled a few meters away from the shop, keeping close to the wall. The town looked smaller than he'd imagined. He'd thought the curb might be a problem, but there was almost no difference in height between the sidewalk and the street. The dragon made it down on the first try, barely teetering. He saw no buildings higher than two or three stories, and though the constructions seemed of better quality and were much more modern than those in Antigua, they looked square and simple. When he turned left to be sure no cars were coming before he crossed the street, he discovered the sea. The sea? It was too extraordinary a thing to be the sea, or at least the sea as he knew it. This was a green and luminous mirror, framed by snowy white mountains. Marvin stayed there awhile, just looking. The faint golden lights of the town edged the shore and climbed a little way up the foot of the mountains.

A truck turned very near the kentuki, and Marvin snapped out of it. He crossed to the other side of the street and went down toward the port. What Marvin wanted, what he would have asked for if someone offered to grant him a wish, was to reach the snow. But a kentuki couldn't climb in the snow, and though the mountains looked close, he knew they were miles away. He took a boardwalk to his right. The beach started a few meters away. Marvin regretted that he couldn't pick anything up with the kentuki—there were shells and lots of different-colored pebbles. He would have liked to bring a souvenir to Lis, to find some way of thanking her for his freedom. On the sidewalk across the street, the door of a bar opened and two men came out singing, holding each other up. Marvin didn't move until he was sure they were far enough away. He went half a block farther, and then someone picked him up. It was a quick, unexpected movement. Marvin moved the dragon's wheels, tried to turn one way and then the other. A masculine voice spoke to him, but the tablet didn't translate. He remembered the tag Lis had stuck on him—was someone reading it now? Everything was upside down, and then suddenly the screen went dark. It seemed the person had put him into a bag and was walking. He waited. Even if he was set free later or managed to escape, now he wouldn't know how to get back; he'd be completely disoriented.

He tried to calm down. He told himself there wasn't much he could do. He heard voices calling him to dinner, and for the first time since he'd started with the kentuki, he thought about taking his tablet with him. It was very risky. Maybe he could take it to his room, hidden inside one of his notebooks, and try to return to the dragon after dinner, once all the lights in the house were out. But his father used the study before he went to bed. He always wanted to see Marvin's tablet there, closed along with his books. The desk was the only place Marvin was allowed to use it.

"Welcome to heaven," he heard.

Someone was speaking to him in English. The light came back, blinding the camera, and then an image appeared that was very different from the street. The dragon was back on its wheels. The room he found himself in was large and had a wooden floor. It looked like a dance hall, or a gymnasium—big enough, Marvin figured, to fit all three of his father's cars. When he turned, he found himself facing another kentuki. It was a mole, and for a moment he didn't understand anything that was happening. For a second he even thought maybe the mirror he'd seen his dragon in had been a trick Lis played on him, and that this mole was his true reflection. Then the mole kentuki squealed and rolled away. Then another kentuki, this one a rabbit, came up next to him and gave him a light tap, then sat looking at him. Two legs came and went among the kentukis. Finally they bent down and Marvin recognized the boy with the ring, the one who'd written the slogan "Free the kentuki!" on the appliance-shop window. His hair was loose and he looked very different in a T-shirt, without his coat.

"Can we speak in English?" the boy asked.

Marvin understood, of course he did, but still, how was he supposed to answer?

Then, from the other world, his father yelled his name and warned him this was the second time he'd been called to dinner.

"If I have to come up there . . . !" he shouted.

But he was already climbing the stairs, the wood creaking under his steps. Marvin didn't even have time to turn off the kentuki or the tablet. He closed his books and stacked his things in the orderly manner his father expected to find them in.

They ate in the dining room with the radio on. The table was too big for just the two of them, so the housekeeper placed a folded tablecloth at one end and set a place on either side. She said it was more intimate, and that it was important for one diner at a table to be able to pass the bread to another. Even though at that table, every night, the only sound was the radio, and never in Marvin's life had he seen his father pass the bread to anyone.

When they finished eating, his father went up to the study to take a phone call. Only then did Marvin remember the battery. Never before had he disconnected without first fitting his kentuki on the charger. He had already wandered a lot and used up much more battery than usual. He realized that if no one charged his dragon while he was disconnected, he would never be able to turn it on again.

"Are you all right, Marvin?" the housekeeper asked as she cleared the table.

On the way to his room Marvin paused for a moment at the door to the study. He observed his father through the crack in the door, making sure he wasn't seen. He was leaning over his papers, elbows on the table and his head resting on his fists. The tablet was a little to the side; his father could reach out and touch it, the *On* light blinking atop the pile of books.

Zagreb — Cartagena

• •

GRIGOR HAD SOLD twenty-three "pre-established kentuki connections," as he called them in the classifieds. Some had been bought in under twenty-four hours. Not counting the ones he'd already delivered, there were fifty-three open connections. He published the ads along with the forms detailing their characteristics: animal, city, social strata, age of keeper, activities in the environment. He took some screenshots and uploaded those as well, making sure that the keepers themselves never appeared, and trying to communicate as faithfully as possible the kind of experience each connection could offer.

His father knocked on the door and came in, making as little noise as possible; he set a cup of yogurt on the desk with a spoon and left. By the time Grigor thanked him, his father was already gone. He devoured the yogurt in a few spoonfuls. Either the recipe had improved or he hadn't eaten in hours. Everything happened so quickly these days, and he didn't think his business could last much longer before some law absorbed the gap in regulations. But in the meantime Plan Fallback was going splendidly, and if there were still a few months of work ahead, Grigor was sure he could save up a solid amount of money.

The cards with their codes could be purchased online and downloaded virtually, but he needed a new tablet for each connection, because once the kentuki was installed on a device, it couldn't be moved to a different one. So he bought an average of five tablets a week, and to keep from arousing suspicion, he bought them from different stores around the city. Ultimately, the tablets cost him less than the connection codes, which were already as expensive as the kentukis themselves. Why did they keep raising the prices on the codes? Was it an attempt to balance the market? Were there really that many more people interested in watching than in being watched? There was no need for sophisticated studies of the technology market; Grigor could draw his own conclusions with just a little common sense. Still, weighing the pros and cons of being a keeper or a dweller never left either side a clear winner. On one hand, few people were willing to expose their private lives to a stranger, and everyone loves to watch, to be a voyeur into someone else's life. But then, buying a device meant obtaining something tangible that occupied a real place in the house; a kentuki was the closest thing on the market to having a household robot. Buying a connection code, on the other hand, meant spending a significant amount of money in exchange for eighteen measly virtual numbers, when people so love to take shiny new things out of sophisticated boxes. In the end, an equal price would keep demand relatively proportional for a while, but even so, Grigor thought that sooner or later the balance would tip toward the connection codes.

A message arrived with a new order. Someone was buying

the kentuki he had based in Kolkata, the one owned by a little girl in India's largest Chinatown: *"Humble family, mother and father absent most of the time. Three children between 4 and 7. Three rooms. The kentuki takes daily outings to a day care. Nightly charge beside the girl's bed."* The customer signed off with a woman's name, and at the end was a postscript that Grigor found overly personal: *"It will be the next best thing to having a daughter of my own,"* she said. *"I'll be grateful to you for the rest of my life."* In general, he preferred not to know anything about the people who bought his connections. He simply checked to be sure the money arrived, put the tablet—powered off and fully charged—into a box, and sent it by certified mail to whatever address they gave him.

Sometimes he thought about his room as a panoptic window with multiple eyes all around the world. In reality, it was impossible to have more than six or seven kentukis awake at the same time—the desk wasn't very big and he had only two hands. He had to move the kentukis around their various areas, charge them if they needed it, and have a minimum amount of interaction with the keepers, who had often been waiting hours for their kentukis to finally wake up and do some dumb thing. He had also bought a couple of small cameras with tripods so he could make analog recordings of connections. He'd thought about it a lot before taking on an expense like that. He wondered whether filming the screen directly—instead of paying for a patch for the tablets and saving the images digitally—wasn't a pretty primitive approach. But he soon found that those videos were quite successful in his classifieds; the analog format gave the recordings a homey yet realistic feel. The customers could also see the exact tablet that they were about to buy, and Grigor's hands, which sometimes entered the shot, lent transparency to the whole service. It was like buying a puppy with full knowledge of who had taken care of it and how well it behaved. As soon as he uploaded three or four videos of a given kentuki, the connection tended to be sold within a day.

In the afternoons, his father would sometimes sit on the bed and stare at the screens with a frown. Grigor had tried to assign him some connections—he couldn't keep growing without someone helping him—but his father didn't even seem to understand what the game was about. Although he'd thought about calling in a friend, he didn't really have anyone he could trust. Nor did he want to split the money. There were already others like him in the market, and some of them had much higher sales. He wondered how they managed it, and if there were other legal gaps that had escaped him.

And he had also had an unpleasant experience. Something he would rather not think about but couldn't get out of his head. That little rich kid who'd had a birthday, and who Grigor had imagined lived close to the Cuban beaches of Miramar, was actually from Cartagena, Colombia; the kid barely ever paid attention to him. The family had put his charger in the kitchen, a kitchen as big as the apartment Grigor shared with his father. Two women and a man moved about the house during the day wearing servants' clothes, while the parents fought every time they laid eyes on each other, even in front of their son and their employees. There was another man who also lived in the house, maybe the boy's uncle, and that man sometimes put the kentuki in strange places. He hid it in the parents' master bedroom, making sure to put it somewhere it couldn't escape from, so the parents would be fighting, or fucking, or throwing things, and suddenly they'd find the kentuki, and one of them would toss it out of the room. One day, the man put the kentuki in the master bath, on the shelf full of towels. Poised on the edge of the shelf, Grigor saw the naked mother get in and out of the shower, dry off, sit down on the toilet and spend a while pulling hairs out of her legs with a tweezer. Every once in a while, she peed. It was all very uncomfortable. But the unpleasant thing Grigor couldn't get out of his head had been something much worse, something truly frightening.

It was afternoon. The man called to the kentuki from the main living room. Grigor tried to hide but didn't make it in time, so the man went over to him, picked him up, and put what seemed to be a cloth blindfold over the camera. Though he couldn't see, he could still hear, so he could tell that they'd left the house and gotten into a car. The car drove for some forty or fifty minutes. Grigor used that time to check on other kentukis, always attentive to what was happening. They went down a gravel road. Then the engine was turned off and there was the sound of some dogs barking. A door opened and closed. From the changes in the light that filtered through the cloth, he deduced that they had stopped in an open area and that someone was taking him out of the car. He heard a cow mooing in the distance. They walked awhile, some seven or eight minutes. Little by little a strange murmur grew. A large gate opened and then closed. Now the sound had radically changed. It took him a while to understand; it was deafening, sharp, multitudinous. When the blindfold was removed he saw that he was in a mesh box. He wasn't on the floor: he was floating among a thick mass of chicks that were stretching their necks and gasping for air. They stepped on and pecked at each other, screeched from asphyxiation and fear, pecked at him as well. There wasn't just one mesh box; there were hundreds, aisle after aisle of mesh boxes. The chicks shrieked, some of their beaks had been torn off and the wounds were open and oozing. A thick cloud of feathers flew above the box and in the aisles of the large sheet-metal warehouse. He saw his kentuki's gray and synthetic feathers flying amid the yellow ones. One of the chicks in front of him, or on top of him, or under him—everything was moving so fast—hit crazily against his camera. It had just lost its beak, and in a panic to defend itself, it smeared the camera with blood. Grigor felt paralyzed as he heard it let out another cry, a cry of intolerable terror that was even more ghastly and piercing filtered through his desktop speakers. Finally he yanked out the audio cables and turned the tablet off. The K52220980's connection lasted just twenty-seven seconds more. After that, Grigor took down the classified ad for that kentuki and reinstalled the tablet's operating system. He could use it for a different connection.

Buenos Aires

• •

WHEN HE FINALLY GOT to Buenos Aires, he found out that his uncle had stopped talking. He was met at the apartment door by a nurse, who kindly took his coat and asked how his trip had been, and whether he'd like a cup of tea before he went in to see his uncle. Claudio accepted. During the flight he had imagined himself several times going straight into the room and giving the old man a good hug—he wouldn't get sentimental; he'd even try for some of that black humor they'd always shared—but the nurse put the tea in his hands, pointed him to a chair, and then tried to explain the situation a little: what he heard in the next room over was not the sound of snoring, but rather the only way his uncle could manage to breathe. His body was too rigid, she said, and as he thought about that word, Claudio felt his own body stiffen. Then he thought: He's awake, he's listening to this conversation.

On the floor behind the nurse's chair he saw a charger. It looked like the round base of his electric kettle, the one he'd bought as soon as he got to Tel Aviv. Then he remembered that about three months before, at the same store where he'd bought that kettle and at the recommendation of an insistent sales clerk, he'd bought a kentuki for his uncle and sent it over with an acquaintance. He hadn't spoken to the old man since.

The nurse went on.

"I don't think he'll make it through the night," she said, looking at her watch. "My shift ends in twenty minutes, and before I go I need to explain some things to you."

Claudio set the teacup on the table.

The nurse showed him where the morphine was and how to inject it. She gave him her contact information and the emergency numbers in case anything happened, although she suggested, very delicately, that it was time to let him go. She gave Claudio an envelope that his father had left for him the week before, when he had also passed through Buenos Aires to say goodbye to his brother.

"Your father said this is everything you'll need for the funeral."

Only then did Claudio understand that the final arrangements would also fall to him. The dark knot that had crept up on him in the airport and that was stuck between his throat and chest now threatened to strangle him. He sucked in air and pushed it back down. He told himself he'd deal with the knot another time.

The nurse left and Claudio stood for a while in the middle of the living room. He realized that it wasn't so easy to run into the other room and give his uncle that hug. He heard him snoring, or breathing, and now that he knew what the sound meant, it was hard for him to stand it. It grew louder at times, as his uncle was consumed by a lack of air.

Another sound distracted him, and instead of going into the sickroom, he headed for the kitchen. Apparently the nurse had left something on. It was a soft and intermittent sound. When he saw the kentuki, he understood. In Tel Aviv he'd even seen people out strolling the boulevard with them, but he'd never noticed the sound they made as they moved. The kentuki was hidden under the small breakfast table. He crouched down, called to it and snapped his fingers, but instead of coming over, the kentuki rolled off in the other direction. The small digital display between its hind wheels was blinking red, but it seemed to have no intention of going to its charger. Instead, it hid out in another corner of the kitchen. Claudio found it strange, but what did he know about these toys. He went closer again, and the kentuki looked at him without moving; it had nowhere to escape to. He touched it with one finger, tapping it lightly on the forehead. He had never looked at one closely before, and he wondered what his professors of nanotechnology at the Weizmann Institute would think if they knew that, in a fit of nostalgia and tenderness, he had given his uncle a gadget like this.

He went back to the living room, and his uncle's breathing drove him over to the sliding glass door and out onto the balcony for a moment. The hoarse sound now reached him from the bedroom window. There was a railing made of two wide wooden beams that didn't reach all the way to the floor. Claudio leaned against it and looked down at the tips of his shoes peeking out over the edge. It was something he had always done on that balcony, ever since he was little. The cars waited at the traffic lights on Avenida Cabildo below. He missed Buenos Aires, and as he stood there on the balcony, he also missed his new city. According to Google Maps, he lived 12,2111 kilometers from his childhood home, but his childhood home hadn't existed for a long time now.

It was hard to go back to the living room. Once inside he could no longer find any excuse for delay, so he peered into the bedroom. His uncle's body lay under blankets that were pulled neatly up to his chest. His head arched strangely backward in the service of his snore. Claudio stood for a while on the threshold, surprised by how silent his own breathing was. Finally he took a step toward the bed.

"Hi," said Claudio.

He said it because he thought his uncle couldn't hear him. Then the man's right hand lifted up toward him and its open palm called him closer. Claudio swallowed hard. He brought a chair over and sat next to his uncle.

"I like your kentuki," said Claudio.

And in a movement that was clearly excessive in his condition, his uncle raised both hands and reached them toward the window. A slight grimace appeared on his skeletal face, and then both hands fell, defeated, to either side of his body.

"Do you need more morphine?"

It was perhaps the first time in his life that he'd uttered that word. His uncle didn't say yes or no, but from his rattled breathing Claudio knew he was still alive. Why would he have gestured so desperately toward the window? He leaned back in the chair and looked around. The shelves, chairs, and tables, normally piled high with his uncle's books and sheet music, were now spotless surfaces covered with jars, pills, cotton, and adult diapers. On the nightstand, the sole personal object in the room was almost touching the pillow: a metal box barely larger than the palm of a hand. Claudio didn't remember having seen it before, and he thought it looked like some sort of souvenir from an exotic Middle Eastern city, the kind his uncle had always longed to visit. Though he was tempted to pick it up, he didn't—he didn't want to disturb his uncle. He sat there some twenty minutes longer, still smelling the airplane food on his own body.

When his uncle stopped breathing, his toes, at the other end of the bed, tensed up. Claudio jumped to his feet and away from the bed. For a while, neither of them moved. Then the silence calmed him, and the sound of traffic on the street returned little by little. He called the funeral home; they would take care of sending a doctor for the death certificate in a few hours, and they would collect the body that night. He went back over to the bed and pulled the sheet all the way up over the body. It was strange—he'd been sure this death was going to hurt, but he couldn't feel anything.

He picked up the little metal box and opened it. He vaguely heard the kentuki's motor as it moved around the kitchen. Inside the box were handwritten letters. They could have been in Arabic or Hebrew, Claudio really couldn't tell the difference. Every once in a while, between one paragraph and another, his uncle's name appeared, written in letters he could recognize. There was a small plastic ring, like a party favor, and it was broken. Behind the letters he found photographs. They were of a boy around twelve years old. He was always the same age and they were taken in what could have been his room or on the patio of his house, and they seemed to be current. He was a handsome boy with chubby cheeks and dark skin. He held up for the camera objects that—as Claudio gradually understood—evidently his uncle had been sending him. In the last one, his parents, their eyes wide and shining with joy, were laughing and holding up his uncle's Yamaha organ, one at either end; at the keyboard, the boy was excitedly pretending to play.

He felt the dark knot again. He put the box down and left the room. He needed to breathe. He crossed the living room and went back to the balcony. He leaned against the railing, feeling suffocated, and stared out at the cars on the avenue below. Only when he noticed that the traffic was stopped in one spot did he see the kentuki. It took him a second to comprehend what he was looking at, but in the end there was no doubt about it: his uncle's kentuki had crashed to the street eleven floors down, very near the sidewalk. Two women were directing the cars so they wouldn't run over the remains. They were trying to pick up the pieces while some pedestrians looked on in horror. The connection of the K94142178 had lasted for eighty-four days, seven hours, two minutes, and thirteen seconds.

O a x a c a

• •

SHE'D GOTTEN USED to moving around the room with the
soft sound of Colonel Sanders behind her. Sometimes she let
him come with her to the residency library. This past week,
even, she had let the kentuki follow her to the terrace that
looked out at the mountains, where Alina would lie on a
lounge chair and sunbathe. They were short trips without
stairs, and she liked that the kentuki could move on its own,
liked to hear its well-won independence at her heels. Sometimes she heard it move under the lounge chair, and she
thought maybe the sun had blinded the camera and whoever-
he-was couldn't see well. She liked that the crow took refuge
under the shade of her body. More than anything, she had to
admit, she loved to have it there waiting for her and to sporadically hear the little motor whir as it moved to follow the
movement of the sun. Its effort relaxed her.

"Are you all right, honey?" her mother had asked her that
morning.

It was the first time her mother had called her in Oaxaca.
She said she had read Alina's e-mails and gotten a strange

feeling. Alina reassured her she was fine, things were going marvelously. Sven, too, yes, yes, the show would be in three weeks.

"And your little friend?"

Her mother always asked about pets, especially when she suspected it was better not to talk about other matters.

"You don't have to service it at all?" she'd asked.

Did she mean give it food and water? Cut its claws and take it out to pee?

"It's a cell phone with legs, Mom."

"And what are you supposed to do with it, then?"

Alina explained what a kentuki really was, how when it was first connected the device's IMEI was linked to a particular kentuki dweller, and how the link to a single keeper was preserved. Her mother was silent for a long time, so Alina tried to clarify further:

"The IMEI is an identification number, any telephone has one. Yours does, for example."

"Is it a number I choose? I don't remember ever choosing any number for my phone."

"Oh, it doesn't matter, Mom," said Alina impatiently.

"So why don't I buy another kentuki and send it to you? That would be nice, wouldn't it? That way we could spend more time together."

"You can't choose who you connect to, Mom. That's the beauty of it."

"Then what's it for?"

"Oh, Mom!" said Alina, though the question got her thinking.

She went to the library almost every morning now, after

she got back from her run and took a shower. She ate lunch while she answered e-mails or read the news. When she was washing dishes in the small kitchen before lying down for a while, Colonel Sanders would tap against her feet, looking up at her and emitting his metallic little cries. The gesture was somewhere between funny and depressing, and it didn't take a genius to understand that whoever-he-was was desperate for a little more attention. He wanted her questions, wanted a way to communicate, he wanted Alina to listen to what he had to say and for her to "service" him. But Alina wasn't going to give in. Without a way of communicating, the kentuki was relegated to the simple function of a pet, and Alina was determined not to cross that line. She turned off the faucet, looked for some tangerines, and discovered there were none left. She would buy more at the fruit stand. She put away clothes and straightened her things, careful not to trip over the kentuki. The day before, she had accidentally kicked it and sent it rolling head over heels, and the crow had lost its plastic beak. She'd picked the Colonel up and set him back on his wheels. The kentuki didn't move for a good while, and it wasn't the first time he'd acted offended.

The truth was, if Alina had understood better what exactly a kentuki was, she wouldn't have bought a device and been a keeper, she would have chosen to dwell in a kentuki. Without a doubt, she was more suited to that condition. Though in the end, if you can't choose your parents or your siblings, why should you have the freedom to choose which side of a kentuki to be on? People paid for someone to follow them around like a dog all day; they wanted a real person begging to be looked at. Alina closed the drawers and flopped on the bed. She heard the kentuki's motor as it came closer, and she languidly let her hand fall. The Colonel gently pushed against her palm, and his plush body brushed her fingertips. She felt for the empty space where the nose had been and scratched it with her fingertips. She let her arm go again, and the kentuki turned softly around her hand, as though petting itself.

Dwelling in a kentuki, thought Alina, was a much more intense experience. If being anonymous online was the maximum freedom for any user—and, what's more, almost impossible—how would it feel, then, to be an anonymous actor in someone else's life?

Later, they went out onto the terrace. Alina spent a while reading in the sun on the lounge chair, then put the book on the ground, took off her cover-up, and lay back in her bikini. Colonel Sanders came out from under her chair and moved farther away, as if wanting to take in the full view of what she was doing. He spent a few minutes like that, until Alina turned over onto her stomach and let her eyes close. She heard the kentuki roll away, then come back closer. By the sound she calculated the Colonel was underneath her, but he was moving suspiciously slowly. He didn't hit against the chair legs like he usually did, but rather moved along just beneath her body. She sensed him under her stomach, advancing toward her breasts so slowly that Alina opened her eyes, though she was careful not to move. She waited. In the distance, a motorcycle silently plied the only line of asphalt on a mountain. Then she heard the kentuki turn a little to the left. The plastic material of the chair tensed, and the kentuki's head softly brushed against one of her breasts. Alina jumped up. Colonel Sanders was motionless, and it took her a few seconds to remember she was barefoot and realize the flagstones were burning her feet. She cursed as she looked for some way to protect herself, and she moved a little farther off where she could stand on the grass. They stared at each other for a moment. Alina decided not to go back for her books and clothes. She went hopping on tiptoe back to the room, closed and locked the door behind her, and stood in the middle of the room, waiting.

A few minutes later she heard the soft, slow taps of the kentuki against the door, summoning her. She had a terrifying image: Colonel Sanders as a naked old man sitting in a bed with damp sheets, controlling the kentuki from his phone, tapping at her door, eager to touch her again. It was a repulsive sensation, but she closed her eyes and made an effort to focus on it, to see it all clearly. She grimaced in disgust and balled her fingers into fists. And yet, with an urgency she couldn't explain even to herself, she leapt for the door and opened it. The Colonel was at her feet; his head turned up toward her as he came in. Alina closed the door and walked around him, the way he usually circled her. She reached behind her for her bikini string and pulled.

"Look," she said.

Her top fell to the floor. It was the first thing the kentuki saw when it turned toward her, and then it raised its eyes to the height of her chest.

"You want to touch them?"

Alina wondered how exactly they would do that. When she'd turned on the kentuki for the first time, she had never imagined this situation, but there was a certain logic in which she continued to trust. She didn't feel like she was imposing on either of their privacy. Whoever-he-was could take photos, keep screenshots, he could jack off inside a felt-covered plastic crow. But unlike the crew at this residency, she wasn't an artist of anything, much less a *maestro*. And being nobody was another form of anonymity, one that made her just as powerful as him, and she wanted to make that very clear. She knelt down on the floor and let the kentuki come closer. She imagined herself with the old man in that damp bed. What kind of things would the old geezer like to do to her? She had never seen any porn with old people. She reached over to the desk and felt for her tablet. Nor had it ever occurred to her to look for porn with kentukis. She opened the search window and typed in *porn, old, dick, kentuki*. She got more than eight hundred thousand results. Were there really that many people fucking kentukis? Could such a thing be done? She chose a video at random, and while it was loading she sat with her back against the side of the bed, picked up Colonel Sanders, and set him on her crossed legs. She turned him so he was looking in the same direction she was, and she calculated how far away she should hold her tablet so both of them could see it well. On the screen, a girl adjusted the camera above the bed. She lay down, and her tits were so big they fell to either side. She reached over for something on the nightstand: it was a kentuki, though it had too many things attached and Alina couldn't tell which animal it was. There was a fluorescent horn fastened between its eyes. A big latex dildo hung from its belly, attached with a belt. And where the ass would be— if those creatures had asses—someone had painted a big red heart. Did the whoever-it-was in that poor kentuki know what they'd done to it? Was the dildo within its camera frame? Then the mattress trembled, shaking the girl and the well-hung unicorn, and a naked old man on his hands and knees entered the shot from the right. Alina paused the video. She didn't know if she wanted to see what came next, but she'd just gotten an idea for something that would finally pull her out of her malaise. She took one of the benches from the kitchen and carried it to the middle of the living area. She put the kentuki in a small ceramic bowl, head down, so it couldn't move. It fit like a ridiculous little hat, but it held the crow firmly. She put the bowl on the bench in front of her open tablet. She made a few adjustments to be sure the kentuki could see perfectly, arranging things so that the video was all it could see. Then she pressed *Play* again. There were still thirty-seven minutes of action left, and there was nowhere the Colonel could escape to.

She got dressed, picked up her keys, and left, slamming the door. Outside, dusk was already starting to fall and the lights were on in some of the studios. If she didn't hurry she wouldn't get to the library in time, and she wanted to see Carmen. That was what she most needed now, someone real to whom she could say something, anything.

She didn't see Carmen at the front desk, so she rapped her fist lightly a few times on the wood. Carmen bounced up into view, loaded down with papers; she'd been organizing the space under the counter.

"That's how you order a whiskey, my dear," she said. "Not a Jane Austen novel." She stood looking at Alina a few seconds and then dropped the papers. "Are you all right?"

Carmen looked her up and down again and then glanced at her watch. She told Alina to wait for her a second and they could leave the residency to get some air.

They walked to the street. Alina wanted the walk and she wanted the company, but she wasn't ready to talk about what had just happened to her. She was pleased to find that the sun no longer stung and a warm breeze was blowing up from Oaxaca. Toward the center of town, in front of the church, there was an open-air kiosk that acted as both a pharmacy and an ice cream and coffee shop. It was the closest thing the town had to a café, and it was still open. The attendant came out right away to clean off the only table on the sidewalk, and they both ordered coffee.

"There's no rest from that damned kentuki," said Alina suddenly, stirring her cup. "I can't stand it anymore. It's depraved."

"You don't like Colonel Sanders anymore?" Carmen closed her eyes and leaned her head back to catch the last rays of sun. "You can always just throw them off a cliff, right?"

That wasn't what Alina wanted. She wanted to rest, she wanted to be the one who decided when the little beast could move around the room and her life. It was outrageous that the keeper couldn't impose a schedule on the kentuki.

They talked about books and ordered another round of coffee.

"Have you seen that?" Carmen pointed inside the kiosk.

On the TV screen, the six o'clock news was opening with a kentuki on the table.

"They turn one on every day."

The two journalists were making signals that the kentuki obeyed, as if it were a dog being trained.

Carmen explained: "If you call in to the program and can prove it's you moving the kentuki, you win half a million pesos. Just like that, they give it to you the same day."

Alina bought more tangerines before heading back, and Carmen bought ice cream pops for both of them. They walked awhile in silence, each struggling with a dripping dessert.

When Alina got back to the room, the kentuki wasn't there. Sven had come by and left again, she could tell from the clean cups and open windows—ventilation was one of the *artiste*'s great passions—but in particular because the bench where she'd left Colonel Sanders was under the table and her tablet was on her side of the bed. Sometimes Alina moved things around just for the pleasure of it, and at first the *artiste* had noticed and moved things, too, to show her he was capable of understanding what she was up to, even if only abstractly. It was an affectionate way of teasing each other. She would close the windows on him, move his shoes to the other side of the bed and leave her own sandals where his shoes had been. She replaced the toothpaste with a cream from the medicine kit, changed the order of some notebooks that he always kept neatly on his nightstand. Sven responded with much less ingeniousness, so little that sometimes Alina had to make an effort to notice. Oh, she remembered thinking, he moved my brushes from the bathroom counter into the kitchen, how clever. Sometimes she wondered if she hadn't done it herself in a moment of distraction. Now she smiled nostalgically in the middle of the tidy living room, wondering if the kentuki's absence might not be a signal from Sven—a way, though very removed, of trying to shift something.

Alina went back out. The idea of Sven and the kentuki

alone together worried her because of how fast the *artiste* could break the long project of noncommunication she had been building: all it would take was for Sven to show the crow a paper with an e-mail address to transform her subjugated fantasy pet into the reality of a dirty old man. She went down toward the common areas and crossed the central kitchen and rec room. At that hour, the traffic of artists reached its peak. They played foosball, they dozed in front of the large projector screen on a massive sofa. They ate standing up with the refrigerator door open, and they sacked the pantry. Squeezed into a hot-pink velvet outfit, Sven's assistant twirled her curls while she chatted with the Russian sculptor who'd arrived the week before. Alina went through the last room, where a group of people were shouting their bets around two dragon kentukis that were competing in a race toward the main picture window.

Alina crossed the exhibition gallery. They had taken down the installation of transparent burkas by the French Afghan woman from New York, and for the first time the space looked wide and open. She went out to the studio area, where some artists were still at work. The crazy woman who made cork installations was singing reggaeton, using what looked like a flashlight as a microphone. In the next room the Chilean photographer couple were working, leaning over a giant print, each of them cutting an area with a razor. Alina passed two more studios and stopped in front of the door to the last one. A small sign said *Sven Greenfort*. It was his handwriting. She knocked before going in. No one answered, so she entered and switched on the lights. The place was clean and tidy, as expected. The wood blocks for printing were lined up by size against the window, and a large number of two-color mono-prints were drying on the main table. What she didn't expect to find were those three boxes on the back table. Three white boxes, just like the one Alina had taken the Colonel from. They were empty. Beyond them, alongside the rollers, she saw a kentuki user's manual. The other two manuals seemed to have met a different fate—their pages were also on the table, torn apart by hand and each one stamped, in red ink, with a fingerprint like all his artistic interventions. That's how poor Sven had worked ever since she met him: though he occasion-ally got up the nerve to experiment a little beyond his limits when he was in his private space, he only ever showed his usual monoprints and xylographs—big and gray enough to hide any mediocrity—while he denied his true desire "to shake up the market." Alina left the studios and went back toward the rooms. Where were Sven and the Colonel? Shouldn't Sven have told her he was working on a project with kentukis? Suddenly that infidelity mattered much more than the one with the as-sistant. She crossed the path to the pools. The cries of the crickets came down from the mountains, furious. She could feel how they lodged in her ears.

Umbertide

· ·

AFTER WORK, Enzo watered the plants in the greenhouse and cut some parsley for the meat. He took longer than usual, waiting for the mole to come out and look over the basil and peperoncini. But the screen door never opened, and in the end he got tired of waiting and went inside to make dinner. He called Luca in to help him set the table, and they ate while they listened to the news. When a short report on kentukis came on, the mole came out from behind the sofa and rolled under the table. It was the first time Mister had made himself known that day, and it had been the same all the previous week—things were no longer going well between them. Mister hadn't at any point neglected his responsibilities as co-parent, but since that disastrous Sunday when Enzo tried to communicate with him, the mole consistently avoided him. How could he be so annoyed at a simple attempt to converse as equals? Would he really rather crawl around the house as a mole than strike up some kind of friendship with Enzo? They were both alone and they spent a lot of time together, and sharing a few beers—even if it was at a distance with a phone in hand—couldn't do anyone any harm. Enzo couldn't understand why he himself was so mad about it, though. Why he felt disappointed and offended by a snub from a gadget less than a foot tall. And still, he couldn't stop himself from doing everything possible to reconcile with the little guy; it was unbearable. He turned on the RAI when it was time for the programs he knew Mister was interested in; he propped him in the back window of the car on every trip to the super-market or to pick up Luca; he constantly checked to make sure the boy hadn't hidden Mister's charger again. While he got Luca ready for school, when he made food or sat down to do a little paperwork, he was constantly talking to Mister and asking him questions. How are you today, Mister? Are you going to go outside a while? Do you want to watch some more TV? Do you want me to open the window? Sometimes he wondered if he might not be talking to himself. Mister ad-dressed Enzo only to let him know when the boy fell asleep in front of the TV, that he wasn't doing his homework, or that, even after his bedroom light was turned off, he was still awake, playing with his tablet under the covers.

News about kentukis was the only other thing that inter-ested Mister. Now, on the Umbertide news, a journalist was reporting in front of a state hospital: an elderly woman had had a heart attack and her owl kentuki had saved her life by calling an ambulance. In thanks, the woman had asked for a bank account number and had deposited ten thousand euros, but then the kentuki's dweller had disappeared, and hadn't been there for the woman's second heart attack, which had carried her definitively to the other world. "Does the kentuki bear some responsibility?" the reporter asked the camera.

"And if it does, what kind of legal action could be applied to these new, anonymous citizens?" A brief roundtable debate opened up in the studio, where one doctor who kept a kentuki in his office in Florence told of a different medical case, and another man who dwelled in a kentuki at the reception of a hotel in Mumbai put forth his own dilemmas.

In front of the TV, the mole was motionless. Luca finished his food, and when he passed the kentuki he gave it a soft and precise kick that was enough to knock it over and send it rolling toward the sofa. The boy kept going to his room. Enzo went over and set the mole back up on its base again. He stayed kneeling in front of it.

"What's wrong, Mister?" They looked at each other. "Was it so terrible of me to give you my phone number and want you to call me? Forget about it, if it bothers you so much, you don't have to call."

The kentuki turned away. Enzo sighed and went to collect the dinner dishes.

The next day, his ex-wife came to see him. It wasn't a visit he was expecting.

"I'll let Luca know you're here," said Enzo in the doorway, without inviting her in.

She stopped him with a hand on his arm.

"No, no. You and I have to talk, Enzo. I'll say hi to Luca later."

He let her in and poured coffee. While he was carrying the cups into the living room, he saw her moving around the house, looking at the floor and in the corners. Then she opened the curtains and peered out into the garden. Enzo imagined she was impressed by how healthy the greenhouse was, and he thought she would surely say something, but she came back without a word and sat down next to him. Her worry seemed genuine.

"Where's the kentuki?" she finally asked.

"It's usually around here," said Enzo, kneeling down to look for Mister under the sofa.

They were sitting right on top of the kentuki's hideout, and Enzo knew it. But he'd just realized that his ex had never seen the mole, and he wasn't sure it was a good day to introduce them. He saw the kentuki motionless with its back to him, hiding behind one of the sofa legs. From where Enzo was looking, there was no way of knowing if it was awake, or if Mister could hear what was happening.

"He's not here," he said, sitting down again. "At this hour he's usually watching over Luca's nap." He handed her a mug of coffee. "He adores Luca, follows him around, and it's a relief to know there's someone else nearby looking out for him. I never thanked you for him. In the end he's a big help."

Enzo forced himself to shut his mouth. Why did he keep doing this? Praising her even now, when he couldn't even stand the sound of her horn honking at 7:40 in the morning when she came to pick up Luca for school.

"Enzo," she said in a tone that confirmed the matter was serious. "I know what kind of relationship you have with the toy, Luca's told me a bit about it."

Toy was a strange word, and for a moment he didn't register that they were still talking about the kentuki.

"I want you to turn it off."

Did she mean disconnect it?

"I want you to get that thing away from my son."

Enzo waited. He couldn't refuse a request that he didn't understand.

"I don't know how to say this," she said. "It's horrible."

She rested her elbows on her knees and put her hands over her eyes like a terrified little girl. Enzo waited a little longer, although he knew that if the kentuki moved under the sofa, she would probably hear its motor.

"They're pedophiles," she said at last. "They all are. It's just come out. There are hundreds of cases, Enzo."

She brought her hands down to nervously rub her knees. Seeing her there on his sofa again, it seemed to Enzo that his old drama queen had come back invigorated with new and unexpected tragedies.

"It's a gadget, Giulia. How can it hurt the boy? You don't even know him. We don't know who it is."

"And that's the problem, Enzo."

"We've lived together for three months. Three months."

He realized how ridiculous this argument was, so he stopped talking.

"He could be filming Luca, he could have tried to get into contact with him, said things to him, shown him things, all while you're wandering around distracted in the backyard."

So she *had* seen the greenhouse and been hurt by how good it looked. Enzo tried to smile gently, just to discredit what he was hearing.

"I know Luca hates it, Enzo. He detests it. Maybe the poor boy doesn't even feel like he can tell us what's happening. Maybe he's too ashamed, maybe it's too horrible, maybe he can't even understand what's being done to him."

How had he spent years living alongside a woman who

could think such things? Enzo felt so repelled that he got up and took a few steps from her. She kept listing perversions, and later, after she'd said goodbye to Luca in the doorway, she was still coming up with more nightmare situations.

"I want you to turn it off," she said again now, as a goodbye. "I don't want that thing around my son anymore."

When she finally left, Enzo stood behind the door until he heard the car start up and drive away. He'd open the windows and air out the house. That was what he needed, thought Enzo, a little air, and a beer.

Lima — Erfurt

• •

SHE HAD GOTTEN the Erfurt emergency police number. If the German guy got violent with Eva, she now knew what to do. She still couldn't give an exact address, she knew that, and if the people in Erfurt couldn't understand her rudimentary English, she couldn't do much good, either. Still, she felt more prepared for what might come. She kept her phone close at all times: if something happened, Emilia would immediately record a video of events in Erfurt. She wasn't sure if a home-made video could be used to charge someone in Germany, but if Eva ever needed proof of some kind, Emilia would have it.

Even so, she acknowledged her limitations, and knew that soon enough she'd have to come up with more reliable measures. Klaus—that was the German man's name—no longer tormented her. Her son had explained that the translator didn't work on him because it focused only on the tone of the kentuki keeper's voice. So it was easy to ignore Klaus when he was with Eva. When he wasn't there, she took the opportunity to circulate diligently through the house, attentive to the things that were within her reach and the possibilities they offered. She followed Eva closely, eager for any new information, attentive to anything the girl might say or do that could give her a new clue for her plan.

"You're restless, sweetie, what's wrong?" Eva asked.

If Emilia purred, Eva would stop doing what she was doing and affectionately pinch the bunny's belly. The fact that her keeper thought all she needed was a little love was a practical and stimulating reward.

Before sitting down at her computer, Emilia made herself some tea and turned up the heat in the apartment. The days were getting colder, and she knew that once she was sitting down and tuned into Erfurt, she wouldn't find a moment to get up. She called her son after that day's session.

"I want to send you a photo of Eva," she told him. "She's so pretty."

Her son explained that you couldn't take photos from the kentuki. He said it was a "privacy matter" and that everything was "encrypted." Emilia thought maybe her son was jealous, and she caught herself smiling.

"No problem," she said. "I'll take pictures of the screen, and I'll send you some tomorrow."

Her son was silent, maybe surprised by how quickly his mother had resolved this technological setback. And then, with the hesitant voice of a person making a confession, he told her about his own kentuki. Apparently, when he'd bought the connection card for Emilia, he'd also bought a kentuki for himself, although it wasn't until he saw how pleased she was with hers that he had ventured to turn it on. Also, having his own connection helped him understand more clearly the questions and concerns she posed to him.

"But . . ." said Emilia, when what she really wanted to ask was how long, and whether his was in Erfurt, too, and if they were neighbors now, wouldn't they get to see each other more often?

"Listen to this, Mom. You know what she did yesterday?"

For a second Emilia didn't know who they were talking about. Once he'd started confessing, her son had seemed to lose his fear, and he began to talk nonstop about these past few weeks—a month almost, she calculated—blurting out everything he'd been hiding from her without an ounce of guilt. Emilia carried the phone into the dining room and sat down at the table, like she did when she organized the gas and water bills and needed room to spread out. Her son's voice was telling her that his kentuki had sent him a chocolate ice cream cake for his birthday.

"You gave it your address?" Emilia asked in alarm.

How could so much happen behind her back? Deep down, Emilia was trying to do something with the anguish she felt had gotten stuck in her throat. What kind of mother was she, that it had never occurred to her to send her son a cake for his birthday? Had he thought about that question, too?

"No, no. I didn't give her any address, Mom. The thing is that from the balcony of my apartment, she saw the Young Kee Restaurant right across the street, and she remembered she'd been there when she visited Hong Kong with her husband."

From the balcony of her son's apartment? This was a married woman? She made a great effort not to interrupt him.

"She's old but very sharp." Emilia swallowed. Old but sharp? And which one of those did her son not consider her— old or sharp? "So she figured out the address of my building and sent a chocolate ice cream cake to each of the apartments. There are two in front and two behind on each floor—that's thirty-two cakes, Mom!"

Emilia thought that would cost a lot of money. And it took her even a second longer to realize her son had bought her the connection to a kentuki, and on the other hand, he'd bought a real kentuki for himself, like the one Eva had in Erfurt. Her son would rather be a keeper than a dweller? That is, he would rather *have* than *be*? And just what did that tell her about her own son? She didn't want to learn anything uncomfortable, and even so, if people could be divided between kentuki keepers and dwellers, it disturbed her to be on the opposite side from her son.

"And you know what the funniest part is?"

"What's the funniest part?" She took a deep breath.

"That this poor guy who had to deliver the cakes, who spent half the morning going up and down in the building, also had to deal with a lot of people who wouldn't even accept them. He gave me two extras when he delivered mine."

Emilia took a sip of tea, but it was still too hot.

"So you have three cakes."

Fantastic, thought Emilia. And her son said:

"I'm sending you a photo."

"A photo." Did he mean of the cake or of the woman? Emilia heard a beep, looked at the phone, and opened the image. The woman was a large and robust brunette, standing in the door of a country house. She looked to be the same age as Emilia.

"She was a cook all her life," said her son. "In the Serbo-Croatian war, too, she cooked for the Croatian fighters. I'm sending you another picture, look . . ."

Emilia heard another beep and decided not to open the new photo. Could she send him a gift now, almost a week late?

"It's from the nineties in Ravno, she's looking for anti-personnel mines with the soldiers. Isn't she amazing? Did you see the army boots she's wearing?

Since when did her son have such enthusiasm for working women? As if she, in all her life, had never cooked him anything. Or was it that the sacrifice was worthwhile only if you were sifting flour in the middle of a war and wearing a pair of men's boots?

When they finally hung up, Emilia sat for a while staring down at the table. She thought about going to bed, but still felt too wide-awake. She called Gloria and told her about her son's confession. Gloria had bought a kentuki for her grandson, and they liked to exchange anecdotes. Emilia and Gloria had seen each other at the pool that morning, along with Inés, but since Inés couldn't stand to listen to them talk about kentukis anymore, they saved the subject for phone conversations and left the post-pool sessions for politics, children, and food. If something important happened with their kentukis, Emilia and Gloria said their goodbyes at the door to the club, making signals to each other that Inés couldn't see, promising to call as soon as they were alone. It was fun to discuss their kentuki lives, and more than once they took the opportunity to also talk about Inés, whom they loved a lot, of course, but who lately they'd noticed could be quite conservative. In the end, as Gloria had said in her last call, either you get with the times or let life pass you by.

She'd told Gloria what had happened with the German

man. About his nudity, the money he took from Eva's purse, and how he'd chased her around the living room as if she were a chicken and then stuck her under the faucet. Gloria thought it was a miracle she'd survived—she had a neighbor who'd lost her owl kentuki by leaving it in the bathroom while she showered. She took overly hot showers, it had to be said; maybe the steam was dangerous for the models of animals that weren't native to tropical zones.

"But this thing with your son, I still don't understand—what is it that bothers you so much?" Gloria asked over the phone.

Emilia thought of the last photo the boy had sent, the woman's war boots. She didn't know what it was, exactly.

"Buy one for yourself," said Gloria.

What would that solve? She wasn't about to buy a kentuki. She wasn't that kind of person, and plus, she didn't have the money.

"They're really expensive," said Emilia.

"There are people who sell them used online. Half price. I'll go with you to pick it up."

"I don't want someone else's castoff. Plus, I'm not the kind of person who wants to be a keeper," she said, thinking of the boots of the woman in her son's kentuki. "I'm more like the people who dwell."

She thought about their conversation all that day, and the next. On Thursday, before connecting to Erfurt, she looked through the classifieds for used kentukis. There weren't many, but there were some. Most of them were advertised in the pet section, and from looking at so many animals, Emilia wondered if it might not be better to adopt a real dog or cat, though it was true that a kentuki wouldn't get anything dirty or shed its fur, and she would never have to take it out for walks. After a big sigh, she closed the browser and opened the kentuki controller. Klaus was walking around the house again. Emilia sat up straighter in her chair and adjusted her glasses. She would focus on Erfurt and the girl, who wasn't living her best life right now. She would worry about her own life and her son's later; she had all the time in the world.

Antigua

• •

IT WAS A REVOLUTION. The important things were explained to him nice and clear, and the rest he was figuring out as he went along. The boy with the ring had come up with his plan over a period of months, starting from the first time he saw a kentuki in a shop window. Marvin hadn't been kidnapped, he'd been liberated.

He found this out the next day, after a night spent biting his nails in bed. When he finally got home from school, he ran to the study and turned on the tablet. He woke up the kentuki while he prayed a quiet Our Father, and then God, who in his wisdom was revealing just what was good and bad for Marvin, illuminated the screen. The dance hall shone in every pixel, and every pixel was reflected in his eyes. His dragon was on a charger. He was alive! He needed to move a little, emerge from what appeared to be some kind of box, in order to get a little distance and figure out where he was. Against one of the dance hall's walls, twelve wooden cubbyholes were lined up just beneath the mirror. Two of them were occupied: a mole in one and a panda in another, almost at the opposite end. The kentukis were waiting in place with their eyes closed. Did his dragon close its eyes when he wasn't inside?

The boy with the ring saw him moving and came over to him. He was holding something that looked like squares of cardboard, and he knelt down in front of Marvin and showed him one. It was a sign about the size of a book. At the top it had the number 1. Below, in English, it said:

SEND AN E-MAIL TO THIS ADDRESS.

The boy turned the card over, and on the other side was an e-mail address. Marvin sat studying it, then realized the boy could lower the card at any moment, so he dropped the tablet and started searching like mad among his notebooks, looking for a pen. He wrote down the e-mail address, opened his account, typed **Hello,** and sent the message. When he had finished, he moved his kentuki a little backward. The boy lowered the card and raised another one. This one had the number 2. Evidently, everything was planned and prepared; maybe other kentukis in the hall had gone through the same process. The second card said:

WAIT.

Marvin waited. The boy walked away, typing on his phone, and a rabbit kentuki followed his every move. Soon Marvin received a reply message in his in-box.

Install this program.

An application was attached. Marvin glanced at the closed door to the study and didn't think twice. In under a minute the installation was in process. The controller closed, and when it opened again, there was a chat window on the right side of the screen. There were messages in very strange languages. None were in Spanish, but he understood the ones that were in English.

"Kitty03=in knysna 24°, you owe me $2"

"kingkko=and finally: the sardines. Now that's a no go"

"ElCoyyote=here -5°. Going into"

"kingkko=that's why I left my mom's house, right?"

"ElCoyyote=surgery. I'm taking out a kidney and I'll see you guys later"

"Kitty03= :-)"

Marvin heard another message enter his in-box. It was a confirmation of membership in the Liberation Club. **You're here now,** it said farther down, with a link to Google Maps. He was at 39 Prestevannsveien, in Honningsvåg. Honningsvåg! Where was that? He opened a map on the tablet and located it: Norway. It was as far north in Europe as one could possibly go. It was surrounded by snow. On the screen, the boy raised another card. Number 3 said:

CHOOSE A SCREEN NAME AND SEND IT TO THE E-MAIL.

Marvin thought about it for a moment. He made his decision, typed, and sent it.

WELCOME, said card number 4.

And then the boy turned the card over:

YOUR KENTUKI HAS BEEN LIBERATED.

Kingkko and Kitty03 greeted him in the chat. His nickname blinked, waiting for a reply. He ventured:

"SnowDragon=Hello!"

"Kitty03=I love your name, SnowDragon!"

The others also praised it. A certain Tunumma83 joined the conversation, and a cascade of questions kept Marvin busy for a while. No one knew where Antigua was, or even Guatemala, so he sent a Google Maps link. He gave his age and the name of his school, and he clarified that he didn't have a mother, or any siblings, or a dog.

Tunumma83=but this is 3x better you're in the liberation club! there are people who would die to be in your place.

Marvin still didn't understand what this club was all about. The next day, during the first break at school, he and his friends googled it. His club didn't show up anywhere online. There were others, all small and improvised—it seemed like the idea of kentuki liberation had just been invented. It had occurred to someone that mistreating a kentuki was as cruel as keeping a dog tied up all day in the sun, even crueler if you considered that it was a human being on the other end. Some users had tried to found their own clubs and free kentukis that they considered were being abused.

But why would a kentuki want to be freed? Couldn't they just disconnect, problem solved? Marvin knew that freedom in the kentuki world wasn't the same as in the real world, though that didn't really settle anything if you thought about how the kentuki world was also real. And he had to remind himself that he had longed for his own freedom without once thinking of disconnecting. There were even clubs like his in

Guatemala, and they listed all kinds of abuses, things Marvin would never have thought of. He was surprised when his friends pointed to the item "imprisonment or exposure for commercial promotions," and they still had to explain to him that that was what had happened to him in the shop window where he'd lived for almost two months. *Had* he lived in a shop window for two months? He thought about all the times the boy had tapped on the glass and written his messages of freedom. And even so, Lis had seemed trustworthy and kind, not like someone who would ever have wanted to hurt him.

He spent the following days investigating his kentuki's new home and getting to know his companions. There were chargers in every corner. The boy had made a hole in the dance hall's front door, with a plastic curtain over it to keep the heat from escaping when the kentukis went in or out. More than once one of them got stuck and cried out until someone went over and gave it a push.

Sometimes SnowDragon went on excursions. He circled the building and moved within the "safe zone," which was a radius of two kilometers that the boy had sent him marked on a map. The two kilometers basically reached the other end of town, where the few inhabitants who were out at that hour of the night knew about kentukis—though Marvin didn't think they knew about the Liberation Club—and were careful not to run over them. Nor would they try to take them home for themselves.

The boy's name was Jesper, and he was a hacker, DJ, and dancer. He always had a different girl with him. The girls came and went; they were round like balls when they entered all bundled up, but once inside, wearing loose, light clothing, they dodged the kentukis, and Marvin would sit staring at them, enchanted. If he tapped against their feet, sometimes they would kneel down in front of him and scratch his head. They had blue eyes and very pale skin. Jesper didn't pay too much attention to them; he was always in motion, constantly occupied.

If you deposited €45 in Jesper's account, he would attach an alarm to your kentuki's back that could be activated from the controller. Then, if the kentuki was in danger and you activated the alarm, a siren went off inside the kentuki's casing to call attention to whatever was happening. And meanwhile, most important, a locator was activated and Jesper's map indicated where the kentuki in crisis was. A couple of days earlier, at three in the morning, a certain Z02xxx had gotten stuck on a frozen puddle. If it hadn't been for the alarm, the battery would have run out and the kentuki would have been lost. Jesper rescued it from the ice only seven minutes after the alarm went off, confirming his claim that the service he offered was faster than an ambulance.

Marvin transferred the €45 for an alarm. It wasn't that much for the benefits he would get in return, and there was still some money left in his mother's account. Kitty03 and FURIOUS_cowboy both had cameras on their heads that let them record their experiences twenty-four hours a day, even when they were recharging, and the videos went directly to hard drives in their houses. Jesper was working on a drone now for Kitty03. Kitty03 had money and wanted to buy everything; Jesper, basically, was at her service.

In Antigua, Marvin's friends had found Jesper and followed him on social media. Many of his inventions and applications were ideas that were shared among clubs for freed kentuki. Jesper had uploaded a video of the dance hall when, a few days earlier, six of the kentukis had been playing with a ball. It was lovely to catch a glimpse of a world that Marvin saw only at night, and that seemed so much larger and warmer with natural light. At two minutes, nineteen seconds he glimpsed his kentuki sleeping inside one of the cubbyholes. His friends sent him the link and Marvin spent the afternoon watching it over and over. His kentuki's eyes were closed, and Marvin thought it looked so sweet that he would have paid all the money left in his mother's account for Jesper to mail the little guy to him in Antigua so he could hug it.

On the following nights it had snowed again and Snow-Dragon had gone out into the safe zone to watch the show from up close. In reality, what Marvin wanted—even more than to hug his kentuki—was to be very close to the snow, to bury his kentuki in a nice snowbank, all white and fluffy. He was disappointed to see how fast the flakes melted when they hit the ground.

In the controller chat, Kitty03 wanted to know if his obsession with snow had anything to do with his mother. He had talked about many things, and now his kentuki companions knew more about Marvin's life than his father did, or their housekeeper in Antigua who saw him every day. His new friends were grown-ups who lived in cities he'd never heard of before, but that he'd looked up and marked on his geography map, so his school friends could understand at a glance what kind of people he was hanging out with now.

One night he went out for a spin around the hall with Kitty03. There was a pig at the house behind Jesper's place, and it always squealed when it saw them. Kitty03 loved it; she went to see it every day and had offered Jesper €300 to buy it, keep it on his land, and make sure it never ended up in any oven. Kitty03 had done her homework and learned that at a slaughterhouse you'd get €150 for one of those hogs, and she was offering exactly double. But Jesper said that his business included only matters of kentukis, and she'd have to find another employee to buy and sell farm animals.

SnowDragon chatted a lot with Kitty03. Although the chat was open, the message history wasn't saved, so if they were the only ones connected, there was enough privacy to talk about personal matters. Marvin told her more about his mother, and Kitty03 said his was the saddest story she'd heard in her life.

> **Kitty03=from 1 to 10, how much do you wanna touch snow?**
>
> **"SnowDragon=10"**
>
> **"Kitty03=that's how much I want the pig. talk to Jesper. pay 4 what you want, that's what $$$ is for."**
>
> **"SnowDragon=pay 4 what?"**

Kitty03 said that Jesper could build whatever he needed. With a battery extension and a way to move over the snow, he could get anywhere. Who knows, maybe it was just a matter of asking. So Marvin asked Jesper for a budget. He explained what he needed. Two hours later he had a reply. For €310 he could attach a battery-life extension and fit his wheels onto an all-terrain base—he sent a link so Marvin could see what he was talking about. With Jesper's accessories he could go wherever he wanted, take long excursions in a world where he could live without ever going down even once for dinner; in fact, he could live without eating at all, and he could touch snow all day long, once he finally reached the mountains.

Three hundred ten euros was nearly everything that was left in his mother's account. He agreed. He transferred the money immediately, and half an hour later he wrote again to say that he would transfer €47 more—the exact amount left in the account—if Jesper would also send a bouquet of flowers to Lis at the appliance shop. It had to be a very big bouquet. Jesper said okay. He said he had a lot of orders in, that it would take him at least a week, and he'd keep him informed. Marvin wrote back to thank him and say that the timing was fine. He just had one more request. Could he add a card to the bouquet? The message had to say: *Dear keeper: I wanted to go even farther. Thank you, SnowDragon.*

Zagreb

• •

IT'S NOT A SIN to buy twenty tablets a week, thought Grigor, though at the rate things were going, it was better not to raise any suspicions. He took Ilica Street down toward Jelačić Square. It was a long way to walk, but he needed to clear his head; and he'd always liked to cross the city following the train tracks. Once he reached the square, he would have seven different stores to choose from. He was starting to have to repeat the online shops where he usually bought the tablets, and Grigor decided that, while he planned a new strategy, it wouldn't be a bad idea to go out and buy them himself. He would buy three in each store. He'd take the tablets out of their boxes and put them in his backpack. If he managed to buy fourteen tablets without anyone realizing what he was doing, he'd have the week's quota taken care of.

Nikolina, the girl from 2C, was helping him administer the kentukis. For a while now, once or twice a month, she'd been stopping at Grigor's door with a Tupperware full of food and ringing the bell until he or his father answered.

"Don't want you two to miss out on a good meal," she'd say as she handed the Tupperware to them.

Why would they miss out on a good meal? Grigor thought she must have a crush on him, so he avoided her whenever possible. Then one afternoon he ran into her as she was coming out of her apartment, and her face was as red as a tomato—she had clearly been crying. She was carrying something about the size of a watermelon wrapped in a black bag. Grigor asked if everything was all right—ignoring her would have been too rude—and then she burst out crying.

"What's wrong?"

What else could he ask?

She threw her arms around Grigor and hid her face against his chest, without ever letting go of the bag. Then she pulled away and opened it to show him what was inside. It was a kentuki.

"He's dead," she said, and her voice broke again. "My little bear."

She'd gone out on Monday to visit her mother. She had baked some pastries to bring and they'd burned, so she left the kitchen door closed to keep the smell from filling the whole apartment. Then she'd found her mother with a fierce flu, and decided to stay with her over the weekend.

"I don't understand," said Grigor.

"His charger was in the kitchen, don't you get it? He banged against the door so much he left a little blue mark on the wood. He's blue, see?" she said, opening the bag again and softly touching the fabric.

Grigor saw that the eyes of the device were closed, and he

wondered if the user had shut them or if they were pro-grammed that way, to die humanely.

"May I?" asked Grigor.

The girl stood staring into the bag. Grigor reached in and pulled the kentuki out. It was the first time he'd actually held one. He had seen them dozens of times, but never held one in his hands.

"I'll buy it from you."

The girl gave him a little shove.

"You don't buy the dead," she said, offended.

She tried to take the kentuki back from him and he deli-cately dodged her.

"Do you need a job?" he asked.

"Always."

Grigor didn't say anything, but he wondered how she'd been able to buy a kentuki if she was so hard up. He invited her into his apartment and showed her his room full of tablets and spreadsheets. He explained what he was doing, how much he made and what percentage he was willing to offer her if she helped him move the active kentukis for four hours a day. He talked to her without ever putting down her kentuki. She nodded. If her eyes landed on the bear, they filled up again with tears. When she agreed, Grigor put the kentuki on his desk and asked if she'd be willing to start that very afternoon.

Now they spent almost every day together, and this morn-ing was the first time he had left her alone in his room. She wasn't his girlfriend, but still, Grigor thought she was the closest thing he'd ever had to one. His father thought they were in the midst of a romance, and he never came into Grigor's room anymore. If one of them opened the door to go to the bathroom or leave the apartment, they found two yogurts on a tray on the floor. The girl was delighted with her new job; she worked with great concentration and spoke only when necessary.

She mostly took care of the upkeep of the already active kentukis. He still took notes on each case, managed the sales, and established the new connections. He liked those first minutes of uncertainty, when he wandered around absolutely unknown places. More than once, when he established a new connection, he came across an old, deactivated kentuki in some corner. He hadn't seen anything like that in his first weeks of work, but he'd started to see some of these used and discarded devices with the new connections. Some were broken, others crushed, some faded. Their eyes were almost always closed. He was most disturbed, perhaps, when he saw discarded kentukis that were still pristine. What had led them to disconnect? Then there was the one he saw after a week of connection in the south of Kyoto: he was nosing around under the bed in the master bedroom and he found a kentuki that was destroyed, literally torn apart, as if a dog had chewed away at its plastic, fabric, and overlay for days. It was the work of an animal in a house where, at least since he'd been turned on, he hadn't seen a single pet.

As he walked, the street became pedestrian-only and then opened onto the square. Grigor went into a Tisak Media shop first. He bought three tablets and paid in cash, then crossed over to the next store. He picked up three more devices and went to the registers. The whole side display window was full of kentukis and all kinds of accessories that plugged into the USB port. They had harnesses that simulated little hands coming out of the device itself, and with them you could have your kentuki light your path with an LED, cool you off with a tiny electronic fan, or even sweep up crumbs from the table with a little brush. It all looked garish and low quality. At the register counter, a kentuki held a plastic tray attached with a harness to its body. When the woman gave Grigor his total, the kentuki moved closer to him and purred. Grigor put the money on the tray and the kentuki brought it to the woman.

"We've got some good ones here," she said, indicating her display window. "Our kentukis have made some happy customers, I can tell you."

She smiled proudly and winked an eye.

Grigor took his change from the tray, thanked her, and left. Even if it were possible to follow up on the devices she'd sold, how could she possibly know that their dwellers were behaving themselves?

By the fourth store the backpack already weighed a ton. He'd have to return for more during the week, he thought, and headed back to the apartment sooner than he'd planned. He said hi to his father, who was entertaining himself by watching the match between Dinamo and Hajduk Split, and went straight to his room, where he could finally drop his heavy backpack onto the desk. Nikolina had set up the kitchen table against the opposite wall, where she was leaning over an array of seven tablets. Her dress showed the first four vertebrae of her spine, and Grigor stared at them as if he were discovering a body part he had never considered before. Something about the shape of those bones reminded him of the old terrified excitement he felt when he watched *Alien* as a boy. And at the same time, in a weird way, also of the soft and invisible velvet of his mother's neck. Nikolina's slender fingers came and went from one tablet to another, waving at the ends of arms that were pale and flexible, like octopus tentacles. How had he been able to work alone for so long?

"Hi," said Grigor finally.

He was frightened by how shy his voice sounded, and here in his own room. Everything smelled good, everything was in order. Nikolina straightened up on the minuscule stool he'd assigned her, and turned to look at him.

"Hi, boss," she said, smiling.

And a second later the octopus had her back to him again, sunk inside her other worlds.

Vancouver

• •

BOTH HER DAUGHTERS were planted firmly in front of the shelf of kentukis. They were at the supermarket, and the two girls were united for the first time in a joint tantrum. The youngest one would turn four in a few months and she wanted her gift in advance; the older one said a kentuki would help her study, that someone in her class already had one and it helped with her homework. In the end they compromised on buying one for both of them, a fluorescent green crow with a Zorro mask.

"Do you promise to share it?" Her daughters shouted an excited "Yes!" "Okay, then, I'll buy it, as long as we wait till after dinner to open it."

At least, thought the mother, they would learn that joining forces had its advantages, although in the long run a discovery like that could end up threatening what little remained of her own sanity.

Outside, it was still raining; they were predicting another week of rain for Vancouver, and she was worried about what she would do with her daughters until school started.

Back at home, while she put the groceries away and heated up the food, her daughters emptied the doll house, pulling out walls and floors, and with a joint donation of socks, they made a bed in what had previously been the kitchen.

"It'll be more independent if it has its own space," said the older girl, peering at the end result.

The younger girl nodded seriously.

They ate quickly, listening to their mother's instructions. Then they asked their questions. Could they take it to school? No. Could it be the kentuki who took care of them on Fridays, instead of Miss Elizabeth with her soggy noodles and overcooked broccoli? No. Could they take it in the bathtub? No. None of those things were possible.

They opened the box in the living room. The younger sister played for a while with the cellophane, wrapping it around her neck and wrists with utter concentration. The older girl plugged in the charger and fit the kentuki carefully onto it. While the connection was being established, the mother read the manual, sitting on the rug with her daughters behind her, curious about the pictures and some of the specifications; they each held on to one of her shoulders, their sweet and nervous breath caressing her ears. She was enjoying this, too, in her own way. When they were like this, it was very much like peace, the three of them together, the girls' giggles and their soft little hands pressing on her arms, reaching to touch the manual and the cardboard box. When it came down to it, she spent her life pushing forward alone, and moments like these always slipped through her fingers.

The crow turned on and her daughters laughed. The younger one ran in place, squeezing her fists in joy and excitement, crinkling her cellophane bracelets. The kentuki spun on its axis once, twice, three times. It didn't stop. The mother went closer, fearful at first, and she picked it up to be sure it wasn't stuck on something. After all, she thought, there's also someone on the other end trying to figure out how to control the thing. But when she set the kentuki back down on the ground, it shrieked, a piercing, angry shriek. It didn't stop. The older sister covered her ears and the younger one imitated her. They weren't smiling anymore. The kentuki spun again on one of its wheels, faster and faster, and the mother felt the shriek echo roughly on her teeth.

"Enough!" she cried.

The crow stopped spinning and went straight for her daughters. The older one stepped aside, and the younger one, trapped in a corner of the living room, pressed her back and her hands against the wall and stood on tiptoe, screaming and terrified, while the kentuki rammed again and again against her bare feet. The mother picked it up and threw it into the middle of the room. The thing managed to land standing up, and without a pause in its screeching, it rolled back toward the girls. The older sister had gotten up on the sofa, the little one was still motionless against the wall. She screamed when she saw the kentuki heading straight for her, screamed in terror and closed her eyes so tight that her mother leapt toward her without thinking. Before the crow could hit her again, the mother reached a hand to the shelf, picked up a lamp with a heavy marble base, and brought it down hard on the kentuki. She raised it a couple more times and hit it again until the shrieking came to a stop. Destroyed on the parquet, the toy now seemed like a strange open body of fabric, chips, and foam rubber. A red light blinked in agony under a dismembered foot while, still pressed against the wall, her younger daughter cried in silence. When the LED light on the K087937525 finally went out, its total connection time had been only one minute and seventeen seconds.

Umbertide

• •

HE WASN'T GOING to let his arm be twisted—if the mole didn't want to take part in the midafternoon ritual of the nursery, then let the plants he was in charge of die. Enzo seemed doomed to abandonment—his ex-wife wasn't the first woman to leave him. He went back inside with a little rosemary that he'd just picked from the greenhouse to finish preparing the meat.

Yesterday, his friend Carlo from the pharmacy had invited him to go fishing. "You're looking worse than ever," he'd said, giving Enzo a few slaps on the shoulder, maybe knowing that, as usual these days, Enzo would refuse the invitation. But now he was thinking about it. For too long, it seemed he'd been worrying about nothing but the boy and the greenhouse. And that damned kentuki—Mister's contempt was poisoning him.

Things had gotten worse since that last day when he'd fought with Giulia on the sofa with the mole underneath them, hiding. When she finally left, Enzo locked the door and gave a long, tired sigh, went back to the living room, and found Mister a few feet away, stock-still and looking him in the eyes, as though challenging him. Had the kentuki heard his ex-wife's detailed exposition on pedophiles?

"Absolutely not, Mister," said Enzo. "You know I don't believe that."

In the afternoon they went out to do some shopping.

"Bring the mole," Enzo told Luca, while he went to pull the car around.

He knew the Mister loved to ride in the back window, and it would put him in an even better mood if it was the boy who went to get him.

On the road, some cars had decals of their kentukis on their back windshields. People also wore the decals as badges on their bags and coats, or they stuck them up in the windows of their houses alongside the logo of their soccer team or the political party they supported. And Enzo wasn't the only one at the supermarket with a kentuki in the cart. A woman in the frozen-food section asked hers if they needed more spinach, received a message on her phone that made her laugh, then opened the freezer and took out two bags. Enzo envied the people who had been able to establish closer communication. He didn't understand what he had done wrong, what was so terrible that could have offended the old guy, and it was clear that his ex-wife's slander had ruined the situation for good. She didn't call again, but Luca's psychologist left three messages asking for an urgent meeting, and Enzo knew that when he finally ceded, Giulia would be at the appointment as well, waiting for him in the doctor's office, baring her teeth in a half smile.

Since he assumed everything was ruined anyway, he had gone back to trying to communicate with the kentuki. He'd shown it his number again, in case the mole's dweller hadn't managed to write it down. Also his e-mail address, and later, already in a bad mood, he'd written down the address of the house on a piece of paper and stuck it on the sofa leg near Mister's usual hideout. But nothing had worked.

When they got back from the grocery store, Enzo turned on the RAI. The mole moved off toward his corner, attentive to the news while Enzo put away the groceries. The reporters were signing off with a local-color piece: while the headlines raced across the bottom of the screen, a field reporter at Line B at Rome's Termini station updated viewers on kentuki news. A line of some thirty people were waiting to consult the *"gufetto,"* an owl kentuki that belonged to a bum. As the reporter told the camera, the owl "responded to all kinds of questions, except ones about how a homeless person got his hands on an owl kentuki." Some of the people interviewed claimed that the owl's dweller was a famous Indian bhagwan. "I came yesterday and asked for a lottery number," said one. "The *gufo* knows all." One woman said: "I come to see the panhandler because he deserves it. It's a brilliant idea." People came with questions, and they also brought white slips of paper with all the possible answers to the questions. They lined up the slips of paper in front of the kentuki, and, after meditating for a few seconds, the owl would stop on the one that said *In seven days*, or *Better to forget*, or *Twice*. Each consultation cost five euros. If the kentuki didn't choose any answer, you had to pay another five to ask again.

"See, we could make ourselves a little money, Mister," Enzo said, and he laughed as he watched the mole.

The kentuki didn't react. It occurred to Enzo that Mister was privileged and ungrateful, and he sat looking at the mole.

"We need to talk," he said. "The way you're treating me is . . ."

He thought about it; he wasn't sure exactly how to describe Mister's mistreatment.

"I don't know what it is, but you just can't treat people like this," said Enzo finally. And then he said: "You spend the entire day in my house, but you won't deign to say a word to me. It's unbearable. Don't we get along okay?"

He felt an urge to kick the mole, lock it in a closet, hide its charger the way his son kept doing. Then Mister would have no one to wake in the middle of the night, no one who would search for the charger and save him.

What he did instead was tell Carlo everything the next day, leaning against the pharmacy counter like he was in a dive bar. Carlo listened to him, shaking his head every once in a while, a half smile on his face. Then he clapped him on the back and told him:

"Enzo, I need to get you out of that house awhile."

They would go fishing. Carlo set a date and time, and Enzo accepted.

"All weekend," said Carlo, shaking a threatening finger.

"All weekend," said Enzo, and he smiled in relief.

Oaxaca

• •

SHE WAS HUNGRY and happily exhausted—she'd run ten kilometers without stopping even once. She showered and then ate while she looked at her phone; a message from her mother was waiting on the screen.

"Are you sure you're ok?"

By then Alina had canceled several video-chat dates. She wasn't avoiding her mother, it was just that her head was somewhere else. She'd fought with Sven and it hadn't been about the assistant; she never said anything about that, or about the fact that, almost a month into the residency, he hadn't gone with her to Oaxaca even once. Nor was it about the dozens of dried tangerine peels that he'd found under his pillow the night before. Could a person be so removed from the world that he could sleep on tangerine peels for an entire week without smelling them? What kind of man was she living with? No, their fight had been all about the kentuki, and they had argued without arguing. Sven had simply stated that he would be taking it with him every morning to the studio, and she had banged her empty coffee cup down on the kitchen table, and things had only gotten worse since then.

Sven had broken the long stretch of noncommunication that she'd imposed on the kentuki, Alina had no doubt about that. She could sense it when the Colonel came back from the studios, in his reluctance as he knocked at the door. It was as if he were exhausted by this last part of the day, the part he spent with the crazy lady of the residency. The kentuki came back alone between six and six-thirty, when the *artiste* considered his workday over and went down to the common areas. Alina wondered if Sven saved the kentuki the three impossible steps it had to climb to get to the rooms, leaving him on the other side of the embankments, or if they said goodbye at the door to the workshop and it was the Colonel who'd found a way to reach her by another route. When Alina opened the door for him, he went straight to his charger without bothering to hit against her even once, or circle around her giving his rusted-crow cries. Alina wondered what kind of dialogue Sven and the kentuki had established, whether the Colonel had told him about the episode when she'd taken off her bikini top, and how Sven had reacted. There's no reason your partner should understand all the things you do in front of a pet, she thought.

She told Carmen about her problem, just to see what she thought.

"You have it on a platter, *manita*. The kentuki can give you a daily report on the studio and the assistant."

It was easy to find out, she just had to give an interrogation of the type "Take a step forward if . . . , take a step back if not . . ." But she was convinced that reaching the most minimal agreement with the kentuki would open them up irreversibly to dialogue, and Alina wasn't going to fall into that temptation.

One afternoon she waited for the Colonel in her bikini, and when he came back from the studios, instead of opening the door for him she went outside to meet him, ready with her sunglasses and book, as if someone she'd been waiting for had come to pick her up. She headed to the terrace and lay face-down on one of the lounge chairs. The Colonel was slow to follow her—maybe he was too tired to sunbathe after his long workday. But she would let herself be touched, and she'd make a great effort to picture the old man's hands with the greatest possible clarity. If the dweller and the *artiste* were communi-cating, she was going to start sending Sven some signals.

Another afternoon she'd put the crow on her lap, and, by the light of the desk lamp and with the help of some tweezers, she'd spent almost an hour carefully pulling out hairs until she'd branded a neat swastika on its forehead. Sven said noth-ing, though it wasn't something that could go unnoticed. Alina left her marks and Sven ignored them so openly that it was clear he noticed them. She couldn't help wondering what kinds of things went on between him and the kentuki while they were alone, whether Sven also feigned lack of interest with the Colonel, or, on the contrary, whether he waited for those moments to pick him up with compassion and give en-couragement and consolation. Did he apologize in both their names if he found the Colonel with a pair of underpants on his head, or tied to a chair so he couldn't reach his charger?

Meanwhile, she and Sven were dancing the slow dance of evasion. She went out to run in the early morning, early enough so they didn't have breakfast together. Then Sven came back at night always fatigued: "An exhausting day," he'd say as he loped wearily toward the shower. When he came out of the bathroom, Alina was already asleep. They had to exchange brief conversation only every once in a while, so the hostility was never openly declared, and then they each could go back to their own concerns.

"I think I'm going to change some things," Sven said one day, and for a moment she thought he was talking about his relationship with her. "I mean the monoprints," he clarified right away. "Having Colonel Sanders with me all day has given me a couple ideas."

And that was all the *artiste* said to her that day.

On the desk, when she was organizing her papers a little, Alina found the crow's beak, the piece that she had accidentally broken off with a kick the week before, and that, though she and Sven had both spent a while looking for it, they hadn't been able to find. She waited for the Colonel to come back from the studios, and she summoned him to her, pointing at her feet while showing him the beak and a tube of glue. Maybe the Colonel thought it was a truce, because he came right over and didn't make her ask twice. Alina knelt down, opened the glue, and spread a line of gel over the inner part of the beak.

"Come on," she said, with all the sweetness she could muster.

The kentuki came even closer, until it touched her legs, and she stuck the beak right in the middle of its left eye.

"The girls are going to go crazy over you," she said.

When she put him back on the floor, the Colonel spun in clumsy circles. He banged against the table leg and then sped away. He didn't go to the charger, but instead hid under the bed. Alina lay down on the floor and reached out an arm to try to catch him, but the Colonel dodged her every time she got close. In the end she had to poke him with the broomstick to get him out. Twice she managed it, but the kentuki went right back under. The third time she caught him, she put him on the stool in the middle of the room. She set up the bowl stand and her phone, and she left a video of Facebreaker playing at maximum volume. It was impossible to know how much the Colonel enjoyed or hated that kind of music, although she was sure that the seven minutes and twelve seconds of decapitations that accompanied "Zombie Flesh Cult," now with a new line in the middle of the screen, would be a most illustrative sort of information for the Colonel. Now that he was leading the life of an artist, she thought, it was good for him to be open to other kinds of experience.

And then there was the afternoon when she didn't open the door at all. She made sure to leave the room long before the kentuki arrived. She went down to Oaxaca with Carmen; she wanted to go to the market—she hadn't gone back since she'd bought the kentuki. They took a taxi from the residency and rode together in the back seat, both windows down.

"My god!" said Carmen.

As if she'd said "Finally," or "This is just what I needed," or "How beautiful." Her eyes were closed. The wind blew their hair up into the back window, where the strands intermingled. It was a nice feeling, and Alina closed her eyes, too, and let her body sink deeper into the seat. They had lunch at El Asador Vasco, across from the zócalo, and then walked up Alcalá to the Temple. At the market they bought fruit and some herbs for infusions, Oaxacan chocolate, fresh cheese, and some silver bracelets that cost them less than ten dollars. Then, too weighted down to go on walking, they sat for a while in the zócalo with two glasses of mango juice.

"Okay. Tell me, *manita* . . . What are you up to now that you're not taking out so many books?"

Alina smiled.

"A lot of things. I keep thinking of my little schemes."

She wouldn't lie to Carmen ever, she'd just decided.

"Is it about your training? In the village they say they see you running like you're possessed."

"It's an experiment with Colonel Sanders, but I'm still looking for the perfect idea," said Alina.

Carmen sipped the last drops of her juice through a straw. She didn't seem intrigued enough to ask again.

In the taxi back, a kentuki standing on the dashboard chirped to warn the driver about areas that were monitored with radar. That way the driver avoided speeding tickets or having to stop at stoplights. A boy who was able to anonymously hack into the street security systems of Oaxaca was behind it all. In exchange, the driver deposited five dollars a week into an account in Haiti. The five dollars wasn't because he was cheap, the driver explained. It's just that in Haiti, it's a fortune.

When Alina got back, Sven was still out. The kentuki was right outside the door, waiting. The beak was still stuck on its left eye, and someone had taped a flyer for the gallery over the swastika: this week the Russian was showing his work. She was invited to the reception at seven, which, of course, she would not attend. She opened the door and went inside.

She picked up the kentuki, pulled off the flyer, and threw it into the garbage, and then left the crow on the counter in the little kitchen. Alina opened and closed the drawers and cupboards; she knew what she was going to do next, though she still hadn't decided how. The Colonel moved from one end of the counter to the other, peering over the edges of the precipice.

"Keep still," she told him.

He didn't calm down, so she got out a pot and put him in it to contain him—he'd asked for it. Now he could spin in circles of only a few centimeters. She found some string, laid the crow down on its side and made several knots between its feet. Two strings a little more than a meter long were left hanging down between its wheels, as if someone had stuck a big tampon in it. She turned off the overhead fan and brought the stool to the middle of the room, climbed up with the crow in her hands, and, after maneuvering for a good while, managed to tie the body to the fan, head down. She stepped back to get a good look and take some photos. It looked like a chicken hung by its feet, and if it tried to move, the wheels bit into the string and made it swing from side to side. The crow shrieked. She opened the second drawer and took out the scissors. They were big, strong scissors, and she opened and closed them several times, wondering if they were sharp enough. The crow saw her and shrieked again.

"Quiet!" she shouted, hoping for its disobedience, which was the push she'd need for her final gesture.

When the crow shrieked for the third time, she reached for the stool, scissors in hand, and in only two clean slashes, she sliced off its wings.

Antigua — Honningsvåg

• •

SOMETIMES USERS Marvin had never seen in the dance hall would appear in the chat. FURIOUS_cowboy explained to him that they were users who had once passed through the club, but who, after being liberated, decided to leave and choose for themselves where they would live. His friend Dein8Öko, for example, had managed to get onto a bus and get to Sweden, where one of his daughters lived. The girl hadn't spoken to her father in three years, but she kept two kentukis in her yard, and when she saw the little rain-soaked mole standing in the doorway of her house, she'd immediately adopted it.

One time, a user Marvin had never seen before suddenly joined the conversation:

Mac.SaPoNja=i have 5 min of battery max. Dog pulled off tracer pls i think im in basement #2 Presteheia street.

Z02xxx and Kingkko were also connected. They sent messages to Jesper but couldn't contact him. Although Presteheia Street was at the other end of town, they tried to help.

Kingkko looked for phone numbers for houses in the area and called them at random. "Do you live on Presteheia? Do you have a basement? We think there's a kentuki about to die— could you go down and look?" Some people who answered still didn't know what a kentuki was. After seven minutes, they lost the connection. Later, when Jesper tried to find him by following the clues of the tracer, nothing led him to number 2 Presteheia; instead, he ended up crouched under the fishmonger's truck, where, alongside a stolen bag of garbage, a stray dog was calmly chewing on Mac.SaPoNja's tracer. Things like that happened every once in a while. The deaths of other kentukis always brought them together. It got them all thinking. And it made Marvin forget about the real world for a while, and the only thing that worried him in that other, boring world: soon his report card would come, and he would have no choice but to show it to his father.

One night, after a long outing with Kitty03, he received an e-mail from Jesper on his tablet: his accessories were finished. Jesper would fit them on that afternoon, and the next day, as soon as Marvin woke up in Antigua, his kentuki would be ready.

"I'm going to touch the snow," he announced the next day during recess at school. "By the time I get home, everything will be installed in Honningsvåg."

His friends no longer talked about asses or Dubai. They listened, and their eyes were attentive, restless with envy. The one whose kentuki was in Dubai had tried to escape; he wanted to "self-liberate." He'd tried three times now, but was caught every time. They'd set up a small fence around the living room that had put him completely out of the game.

"Is there a plan?" his friends asked. "Do you know how to get from the dance hall to the snow?"

He had it all written down. He had a plan ready that would get him at least as far as the town's exit.

SnowDragon=im going out into the world this afternoon

Kitty03=here's to the brave ones :-)

He made the announcement in the chat as soon as he turned on the kentuki. There was a great commotion followed by advice from the entire group. It wasn't until he came out of his cubbyhole and saw himself in the mirror of the salon that he understood how much the new accessories had changed his dragon. Jesper explained how they worked. With the battery-life extender, he had autonomy for almost two days, although this, of course, depended on how much he used the kentuki. Jesper came a little closer and spoke to him almost in a whisper.

"Check your e-mail, I just sent you something."

It was a map of Honningsvåg. There were seven red points marked on it, and the e-mail explained that they were chargers. It was like receiving a map of seven buried treasures. Jesper explained that he didn't share this information with most of his kentukis, because in the long run it would mean exposing them to a dangerous freedom. But when someone had an important mission, the bases could help them get out of danger. Marvin smiled, swung his legs under the desk. This would make the trip much easier. On the screen, Jesper smiled back at him.

"Now, pay attention, SnowDragon."

He showed Marvin how to activate the snow wheels. They

were high, about a third of the kentuki's height, and now the camera had a much broader perspective. It was as if he'd grown.

"Kitty03=well aren't we handsome today, hmm?"

Z02xxx and Kingkko were also there when SnowDragon decided to set off. Kitty03 proposed that he get as far as the plastic curtain and then all three of them would gently push him out; she said it would bring him good luck.

Jesper was waiting for him in the street. One of his girls hung from his left arm, but she seemed to have no clue what was happening. Jesper knelt down in front of him.

"If anything goes wrong, activate the alarm and I'll be there," he said, showing his fists with two thumbs up.

SnowDragon growled in happiness. He went down the slope and turned right.

"Kitty03=touch the snow for all of us!"

"Z02xxx=we'll follow you from here, champ"

"kingkko=<3<3<3<3<3"

Before setting off on his adventure in the snow, Marvin passed in front of the appliance shop window. Though all the sidewalks had wheelchair access and it was easy to cross the streets, it still took him a good while to get there. He kept very close to the wall to avoid being seen by some nocturnal drunk. He found the store smaller and gloomier than he'd imagined it from the shop window. Stuck in among the vacuums, in a lovely turquoise vase, was his bouquet of flowers.

By now it was gray and withered, but it had clearly been a spectacular bouquet, and he was happy that Lis, as if she'd been waiting for him, still hadn't thrown it out. In Antigua, Marvin felt a knot in his throat, and he wondered if he hadn't abandoned the only keeper he'd ever had.

He went down the ramp toward the port, heading for the area where Jesper had marked the snow on the map. Two dogs followed, sniffing him. They tried to bite his wheels, growling and pushing him with their snouts, and Marvin remembered Mac.SaPoNja and feared his adventure would turn out to be shorter than expected. Finally the dogs left him alone. It wasn't easy or fast to cross the town, but he liked to think that, even now that his mother's account didn't have a cent left in it, he could live for a century as a kentuki without worrying about money. He could eat and sleep in Antigua, tending to his body every so often, while in Norway the days would pass calmly as he went from one charger to another, never longing for a piece of chocolate or for a blanket to get him through the night. Needing nothing to survive had something of the superhero about it, and if he finally managed to find the snow, he could live the rest of his life in it without ever feeling the slightest bit cold.

At one point he lost his balance on the new wheels and rolled over the gravel toward the beach. He came to a stop a few meters down. He'd gotten stuck lying horizontal between the rocks, and although his wheels were large, it seemed impossible to stand up. He heard steps behind him—a man was approaching. He made his dragon growl, and the man saw him and came closer. He picked up the dragon and looked at it for a while, turning its wheels from side to side, shaking it as if it were a box of nuts. Marvin wondered if the tag from the appliance store was still between his wheels. Finally the man got bored with him and put him back on the ground. Marvin rolled off immediately, afraid of being picked up again. But the man didn't move, he stayed right where he was for a good while, watching curiously as the kentuki rolled away.

Marvin had always thought that, for his dragon, humans would be the greatest danger. It had never occurred to him that holes, rocks, and ice would be the most relentless in holding him back. He wasn't surprised when he ended up stuck under a truck. With his new wheels, it was difficult to calculate the dragon's height, and at midnight, after he'd crossed all of Honningsvåg and was just blocks away from the road that led up to the snow, he opted for a shortcut and got stuck between the ground and a gas tank.

Kitty03=how's life, SnowDragon?

The situation was too frustrating and embarrassing to reply. He hadn't participated in the chat since he'd left the club earlier that day, though he had been reading it, and he'd seen his name mentioned once or twice already. He was pleased that Kitty03 and Z02xxx were thinking about him. As soon as he had good news, he would chime in.

But now he was trapped, and although he did everything possible to get out, his head seemed to have been soldered to that hateful gas tank. When his father called him to dinner, he had no choice but to pray for the kentuki's life and battery and leave it to its fate.

The next day, as soon as he turned on the tablet, he saw

that the truck was no longer there. Someone had placed him next to the back door of the fishmonger. He wondered if they'd seen him in time or if he'd rolled under the truck when it pulled away. How scratched up was he? In any case, the kentuki still seemed to function well. The only problem was his battery: he had 4 percent left. He looked at the map Jesper had sent him and saw there was a charger two blocks away, and he headed straight for it. According to the directions there was only one service station in the town, and it wasn't far. He crossed the streets without getting distracted, focused on optimizing his energy. Behind the service station there was a small square, and beyond that, hidden behind seven garbage cans of different colors, was a firewood shed. Someone had roughly sawed a small opening. It was empty inside, and some rays of light filtered through the wooden planks that served as a ceiling; the charger was placed in one corner. It looked dirty and damp. His battery showed only a 2 percent charge. He approached without accelerating too much. If for some reason the base didn't work, he was lost: even if he activated the alarm, Jesper likely wouldn't make it in time. He climbed on. On his controller the red battery changed to yellow, indicating it was recharging. Across from him, spray-painted on the wood, someone had written: *Breathe, you're in the liberated zone.* He took a deep breath. He would leave the kentuki there all night, in that safe space, and the next day he would set off with a complete charge, headed for the snow. He finally leaned back in his father's chair. Only then did he realize he was still wearing his backpack.

Lima—Erfurt

· ·

KLAUS STILL OPENED the girl's wallet, and now he made lascivious phone calls while he scratched his genitals in front of the TV. It was a repulsive display, and after a while Emilia would get sick of it and leave the computer to take care of activities around her own house, peeking into the hallway now and then to evaluate at a glance how things were going in Erfurt.

The German hadn't attacked her again, but she knew leaving the man unsupervised was irresponsible. She knew sooner or later the girl would have problems, and Emilia was the only one who could point to the guilty party. She talked about it with Gloria, who lent her a little handheld camera and explained how to use it. It worked as a good insurance policy: she wasn't informed about everything that went on in Erfurt, it was true, but she had a daily record of her connection. If something happened, she would have it on tape and could send it immediately to the police.

Something else had changed—Emilia surmised that Eva was taking yoga classes. It had taken her a while to figure out, but now it was very clear that that was what she was doing on the days Klaus sat waiting for her while he watched soccer and drank beer in the apartment. Emilia would have liked some kind of notification about this new activity, although since Klaus started coming around, Eva had stopped hanging little signs on the chair legs for her, and the communication between them wasn't as fluid as it had once been.

Sometimes, when it was just the two of them, the girl practiced yoga poses in front of the mirror.

"Am I doing it right?" she'd ask. *"How do I look, sweetheart?"*

She looked phenomenal. Emilia chirped excitedly and Eva laughed. Once, Emilia went over to her left heel and gave it a few taps until Eva understood she had to place her foot in line with her shoulder. Though Emilia had never done yoga, three years of rhythmic gymnastics in her youth had granted her a certain common sense, a knowledge applicable to other disciplines.

Often, nearly half the time, when Emilia woke her kentuki it was only Klaus in the apartment, and if she saw the German she was careful not to move or make any sound. She preferred to keep an eye on him while she pretended to sleep. She kept her eyes open, but didn't make any movement or respond if the man peered into her screen. After all, what did he know about how a kentuki really worked? She was sure he'd never read a manual in his whole life.

Sometimes, at Gloria's suggestion, she looked at some of the recordings randomly, just to make sure they were being saved correctly and to know what kind of material she'd have if the time to report him ever came. That was what she was doing one day when Gloria called to ask if she could stop by.

At first the surprise annoyed her—she'd have to hurry and tidy up before Gloria arrived. But then she remembered Klaus and thought how finally she could show someone her little Erfurt, so she agreed and ran to sweep the living room and the kitchen. She gave her bedroom a once-over, and when she passed in front of the computer, out of habit, she glanced quickly at Eva's apartment. She'd moved on to clean the bathroom mirror when it dawned on her what she'd just seen. She dropped the cloth into the sink, and as she peeled off her gloves, she went back to check on what was happening. From the dog bed, the horizontal image showed Klaus drinking his beer in front of the TV; her attention zeroed in on the German's red shirt. It said *Klaus Berger* and it had the number 4. Emilia went over to her wicker chair and sat down at her desk. Under the number it said *Rot-Weiß Erfurt*. She opened a search window and googled it immediately. It was a soccer team, just as she'd thought. The website listed the players, and among them was Klaus Berger, alongside a photograph of a man much more attractive and professional-looking than the one she saw on her screen now, lounging on a sofa. Emilia didn't let herself be fooled: there was no doubt it was the same man. She googled the name separately and found him on several social media sites. Almost all the photos of Klaus were the same: he was holding a soccer ball, or had one arm around a girl's waist, or both arms around the shoulders of other players. Eva didn't seem to be in any of the photos or have a profile of her own, and Emilia realized she was disappointed. Would she have liked to contact her, write her a message? She wasn't sure. What would she say? "Dress more warmly"? "Eat more"? "Find yourself a better man"?

All of Klaus's contact information was neatly listed on the site. When Emilia saw the phone number, she knew what she would do next. It was just that sitting around waiting for catastrophe to strike wasn't her way of doing things; she hadn't raised a boy like hers by sitting around with her arms crossed. She got her phone, entered Klaus's number, and texted a message.

I know you take money out of Eva's wallet, she wrote in Spanish.

And only after sending it did she realize that, as soon as he received the message, he would also have her number. She thought of Inés, who still insisted that having a kentuki meant opening the doors of your house to a complete stranger, and for the first time she understood the real danger it implied. Her phone's chiming ringtone let her know she had a new message, and a shiver of terror forced her to her feet. Could she really already be receiving a reply from that giant German? She thought of her husband, though she didn't really know why. Finally she gathered her courage and reached for her phone. The message said:

She pays me 50 a week in exchange for great sex. Want to join in?

She understood the English, and the message left her breathless for a few seconds. Then the phone rang, her own phone in her own hands. It was Klaus's number. She knew that if she didn't answer soon, it would go to her voice mail, and she imagined Klaus listening to her voice, her old-woman apologies in Peruvian Spanish, her promise to return the call. She was afraid to look back at her computer screen. Klaus could have taken her out of her dog bed while she was sitting here trembling, trying to reread the message over and over without her glasses; he could have finally indulged himself and stuck her under the faucet in the kitchen, or he could have thrown her out the window. Maybe she was already dead and she just didn't know it yet. She left the phone on the table, gathered her strength and turned around to look: the horizontal image on the screen was still motionless. She waited until she was sure Klaus wasn't nearby. She had to calm down. She took a deep breath and waited. There wasn't a sound from the TV; in fact, the apartment was in complete silence. Maybe Klaus was too much of a coward to retaliate, because in the end, any action he took against her would only end up causing him problems with Eva. From where she was she didn't have a complete view of the living room and kitchen, but there didn't seem to be anyone there. The bag Klaus usually brought with him and left beside the door was gone. She sighed in relief. And then she saw it. On the living room mirror, written with Eva's lipstick at the height where a kentuki could have written it—though no kentuki could really write anything on a mirror—it said: *Whore*. The handwriting was terrible. He'd written it in English, and she wondered if Eva would be able to understand it, too. There were still almost twenty minutes before Eva got back, and yet, whatever Emilia might do with her kentuki, she knew it would be impossible to erase the writing by herself.

When Eva came into her apartment, she set her bag on the table and caught sight of her lipstick uncapped and ruined on the floor.

"What happened here?" she asked.

The voice was trying to be authoritarian. Eva came over

to the dog bed and discovered the message on the mirror. Did the girl really think that a kentuki lying on its bed was capable of such a thing? Now Emilia did want to write to Eva, she wanted to shout: "It wasn't me! You have to get that man out of the house!"

"Who did this?"

Emilia moved her wheels, and she had the feeling that if Eva took her out of the bed and she could finally manage to move, she would find a way to explain herself. But Eva seemed too angry. She wiped the mirror with glass cleaner and threw the lipstick into the garbage. Then she sat down in front of the TV in a position very similar to Klaus's, which to Emilia seemed almost like a provocation. The girl reached for the beer that had been left beside the sofa, and she took a sip as she looked uneasily at Emilia out of the corner of her eye. After a while she got up again, came straight over to the bed, picked up the kentuki, and brought it into the bathroom. What was happening? Emilia had never seen the bathroom. A mixture of fear and excitement overwhelmed her in Lima as she sat in front of her computer. Eva set her down in the bathtub and scolded her one last time, then turned off the light, closed the door, and left her pet bunny alone.

Emilia sat stock-still before the dark screen. It would be hard to escape a bathtub, and still more difficult to process all the things that had just happened. She was still sitting there some minutes later, when the sound of the doorbell startled her.

It took her a moment to remember Gloria's visit and get up to answer the door. She smoothed her hair a little and crossed the dining room. She hadn't finished tidying up the house, but now that seemed like an absolutely minor issue. The doorbell rang again, and Gloria called her name and knocked on the door. As soon as Emilia opened it, Gloria came bustling in, carrying a box that she set on the dining room table.

"Open it," she said, with a mischievous smile that Emilia didn't like.

The two of them stood looking at the box.

"Come on, then." Gloria pulled off a corner of the wrapping paper.

Emilia understood right away that it was a kentuki box, already opened and a little scuffed. Gloria took out a charger, a cable to connect it to the wall, the user's manual, and, finally, a kentuki wrapped in a dish towel. She handed it to Emilia with the utmost care.

"It's a gift," said Gloria. "So you can't return it."

Emilia thought about Klaus, and about Eva's rage when she threw her lipstick into the garbage. She thought it was all too much, more than she could manage. When she unwrapped the kentuki, she discovered something absolutely unexpected: it was a bunny, identical to the one she dwelled in, in Erfurt. She remembered she had a strong-enough ribbon in the bathroom, and she thought that if she tied it around the bunny's ears, it would be like having herself moving around her own house. Emilia smiled; she didn't want to encourage her friend, but she couldn't help it, and Gloria was already clapping with her usual enthusiasm.

"I just knew you were made for each other," she said.

Emilia left the rabbit on the table. She wondered how anyone could get rid of such a sweet little thing. So soft and cute. She saw its eyelids were closed, and she realized it had been a very long time since she'd seen anyone with their eyes closed. Years, maybe? Maybe since the one time her son had come to see her from Hong Kong, when he fell asleep in front of the TV?

"He must be resting. But he's all charged up," said Gloria, and she plugged in the base next to the living room door. "Should we have a little tea?"

When Gloria left, Emilia collected the cups and changed into her pajamas. The bunny was still motionless, so she left it on its charger in the living room and went to bed. She woke up with a start at midnight. What had she been dreaming? She could have sworn it was about Klaus, something terrible, though she couldn't remember exactly what. She turned on the lights and crossed the living room. The kentuki was still on its charger with its eyes closed, just as she'd left it before going to bed.

Since she couldn't sleep, she went over to her desk chair and woke up the computer. It was the first time she'd turned on in Erfurt at that hour. She looked at her watch: 3:10 in Peru was 10:10 in the morning in Germany. She was on the kitchen table. It was a spot she'd never been before, and it gave her an absolutely new view of the apartment. Then she saw the charger signal on her screen and understood. Eva had forgiven her. She'd taken her out of the bathtub and placed her on her charger, as her son had told her must happen every night while she slept peacefully in Lima. There was already light in the apartment, and she didn't need to get down from her charger to see the photos hanging on the refrigerator. There were none of Klaus, but in the center, below a calendar, there was a photo of Eva and her, Eva with her bunny. She was sitting on the sofa—the photo was taken from above, maybe by Klaus himself—and Eva held her bunny as if it were a puppy. Her lips were pursed, she was blowing it a kiss, and Emilia saw herself sweetly asleep, her little eyes closed. The tenderness of the image moved her. She picked up her phone and took a picture of the screen. The next day, she would print it and hang it on her own fridge. She'd hang it in the center, away from all those delivery magnets, so she could look at it every time she passed by, the way Eva looked at her.

Sierra Leone—
Hong Kong

• •

HE SAW A DARK NIGHT, and below the night, the hands of a crowd tossing him up into the sky. He spun in the air, fell, and was hurled upward again. On the horizon, the shining teeth of a large city, and in front of him, for seconds at a time, the stage. The music vibrated and surrounded him. Every beat of the bass drums shook the audience in a single quake. He saw the trumpet players, the bass players, the lights, and the cameras crossing between the musicians at top speed, flying over the stadium end to end. One voice shouted and thousands answered, in raptures over their own harmony. Now they threw him into the air. Caught him and tossed him up again. At times there was only the navy blue darkness of the sky. Sometimes, as he fell, first he saw the sea of hands and heads, and a second later there was a face he'd never seen before and would never see again, as he almost collided with the expectant smile. This was more than he'd dreamed of. He wanted to stay there forever, with all those faces that took turns waiting for him and flinging him up again. The shouts and the vibrations, again and again, that loud and velvety voice that was a match for the audience. To be that and nothing else. There was one face that repeated, the large and feverish eyes of a girl who caught him, entranced, and launched him upward again. He spun around, aware that at times the crowd opened up with a dangerous porousness, and that it would all be over if no one was there to catch him. They were on the ground, or on the ground that was sometimes in the sky, and he was in the air, spinning between two worlds, praying for that other life, one that could deliver him.

When he did hit the ground, the music went silent, and the screen blinked for a few seconds before going out. Ishmael fell back into his seat. He waited with wide eyes, because all the noise had disappeared in an abrupt instant, and for a moment he was disoriented: the camp sirens had stopped. The explosions had stopped. The gunshots had stopped. The lights of the nursing tent were lit again. Soon the next shift would arrive and they'd ask him to leave the makeshift office. Above the shack, from the other side of the stream, among the hundreds of white tents and above the hill and the whole Sierra Leone night, the silence was now a dense and suspicious dome; and his hand, rough, still trembled above the mouse.

Umbertide

· ·

IT WAS A GOOD DAY, and the forecast was for sun all weekend long. Enzo had already packed his bag, his one-person tent, and his fishing rod. Now he only had to take care of making breakfast for Luca, who was staring sleepily into his chocolate milk, apparently feeling the weight of the days he'd be spending at the beach with his mother. Enzo had made plans to meet Carlo at nine in front of the rotunda at the Umbertide exit. He was going to bring the kentuki. He knew Carlo would be annoyed—the invitation to go fishing, aside from getting him out of the house, was meant to get him away from the kentuki—but he had a plan, and it seemed infallible. The mole—that little soul hell-bent on not communicating with him because of whatever he'd done to hurt or infuriate it— would soften when Mister saw the calming green flow of the Tiber's water, when he heard Enzo having a nice long chat with Carlo, when he found out who Enzo really was for his friends and Mister could see just what kind of company they could be for each other. He'd become obsessed, he understood that, and the fact that he realized it was proof that the situation was not beyond his control. Deep down, simply, Enzo believed that two lonely people, from two possibly very different worlds, had a lot to share with and teach each other. He needed that company, he wanted it for both of them, and he would end up winning it.

He started the coffee and made toast. The mole, maybe alerted by all the commotion, moved among the bags.

Enzo explained his plans over breakfast, and he didn't beat around the bush:

"You're coming with me, Mister."

Enzo knew the kentuki might worry, since it had never been out of the house for so long, and especially—and he knew this was what could upset Mister most—he didn't like being away from the boy any longer than he had to. The kentuki didn't move. It stopped short beside Luca's chair. It didn't chirp or hit the table legs. Enzo and Luca both found its stillness so odd that they leaned down toward it, father and son, thinking maybe something strange had happened. They heard Giulia's car honking outside and the boy jumped up, grabbed his coat, and hugged his father. He put on his backpack and said goodbye again before he left. From the floor a few feet away, the kentuki was still looking at Enzo.

He picked up a few dishes from the breakfast table and then heard Giulia's horn again—what was happening?—and one of the doors slamming. Luca was coming back, he could see him now through the window's curtains. The car engine turned off and he heard the driver's-side door shut. His ex-wife was getting out, too?

"Dad," said Luca when he was back inside, in an apologetic tone.

"What are you thinking?" said Giulia, who followed the boy inside. "He's going to be gone a whole weekend, and you don't even put a jacket in his bag!"

Giulia wasn't looking for any jacket, that much was clear; she was scanning the floor, checking behind furniture legs and under the chairs around the table. She was searching the house with a hard smile that Enzo knew very well—it was her clumsiest and most disinterested way of pretending.

"Here it is," said Luca, holding up his jacket.

But his ex-wife had already found the kentuki.

"Let's go," said Luca, and he pulled his mother toward the door.

Enzo understood that the boy had lied for him. She must have asked him if the kentuki was still in the house, and Luca had lied, lied for him. For the sake of his father's marvelous friendship with "the toy." Then the phone rang. It rang three times and stopped. And Giulia, who had taken a step toward Enzo to start raging at him over the kentuki, stopped.

"That happens here, too?" she asked.

"What does?" asked Enzo, though he'd understood very well what his ex-wife was referring to.

Luca looked at Enzo, and the boy's round face was now white as a sheet. The phone rang three more times and then stopped. As far as Luca knew, it was the first time this had happened in his house, but the boy's face disturbed him. When the phone rang again, the boy let his backpack fall to the floor, looking scared, and Giulia leapt to the phone and answered.

"Hello," she said. "Speak. Say something, damn it."

She looked at Luca and hung up. Enzo noticed that Mister

had disappeared during the commotion; maybe he was hiding out under the sofa.

"They don't say anything at my house either," she said, troubled by the call and seeming to forget all about the kentuki. "At least, not when I answer," she said, and glanced at Luca, who was staring down at the floor.

Giulia picked up Luca's backpack and grabbed him by the wrist.

"Let's go," she said.

They headed for the door, and Enzo followed them. She opened it and pushed Luca ahead of her toward the car, and then, careful not to raise her voice, she turned back to Enzo, furious.

"I'm going to get a lawyer," she told him. "I'm going to take Luca away from you, and then I'm going to impale that thing in the middle of your fucking greenhouse."

Enzo stood staring at her. There were many things he wanted to say, but the terror he felt would hardly let him breathe. Only when he finally heard the car start up and pull away did he raise a hand to wave. Neither Giulia nor Luca waved back.

He waited for a moment in the living room, but the kentuki was nowhere to be found. He didn't want to keep looking for the thing anymore; he was sick of playing the needy, offended party. He was furious, so furious he felt frozen in place, paralyzed.

"Call!" he shouted in the middle of the room. "Make the damned phone ring!"

What was happening? What was going on between his son and the kentuki? He thought about all the ways he could break it, smash it, and dismember it, and they were infinite. Still, he took a few steps back. He picked up his bag and coat and left the house. He stood for a second on the other side of the door, looking at the wood, the peephole, the weathered knocker. Then he saw it, on the other side of the window. Between the glass and the curtain, the kentuki was looking at him, unmoving.

Zagreb — Surumu

••

THE WEEK WAS ONLY HALF OVER, and Grigor was already out of tablets. He left Nikolina working alone again and ventured back to downtown Zagreb. He went to one of the few stores on Ilica that he had yet to visit, bought two tablets there and three more across the street, at a small phone shop. He felt like it had been a long time since he'd really taken a minute to relax, and he plopped into a chair at a little café table in the sun on Tkalčićeva Street. He felt like he'd just returned to the city after a long absence; he decided to have lunch. Across the street, an older woman who was also lunching alone smiled at him, and Grigor smiled back. He realized he was calm; Plan Fallback had worked out, and when the waiter came over, he felt a hunger so voracious he could have ordered two meals.

At the table beside him, two men were playing cards with a kentuki. The three hands were fanned out before each player, faceup. In the center was a discard pile. If the kentuki moved over one of its cards, it was immediately added to the pile. Those gadgets were everywhere now, so common that even his father seemed to be starting to understand how they worked. They were on the news all the time, in local-color stories or reports on fraud, theft, and extortion. Users shared their videos on every social network, with homemade contraptions that had kentukis attached to drones, riding skateboards, or vacuuming floors. Decorating tutorials, personal advice, miracles of survival after bizarre accidents. A panda kentuki scaring a cat and making it leap into the air. An owl kentuki in a Santa hat hitting seven glasses with the tip of its nose to play the notes of a Christmas carol. It was almost a miracle that there was still no regulation on the use of kentukis. A miracle that was the divine fire of his blessed Plan Fallback.

He finished lunch and walked home. Once in the apartment, he went straight to his room and set the new tablets on the desk. Nikolina turned toward him right away.

"We have a problem," she said.

Grigor was surprised not to see the table covered with tablets. Nikolina worked voraciously, the octopus of long arms and conspicuous vertebrae who had so disconcerted him the day of his first outing, and she usually managed ten or even twelve connections at once without a break. But now there was a single tablet in front of her, alone on the table.

"This girl," said Nikolina, pushing the tablet toward him.

Grigor never referred to his connections by the keepers they were linked to. He didn't work with people, but rather with devices linked to IMEI numbers: cell technologies, hexadecimal systems, and a snazzy block of spreadsheets full of data. Who was "this girl"?

Nikolina held out the tablet so he could see. It was the panda kentuki number 47, if memory served him.

"Something's happened. You promise not to get mad?"

Grigor reached over to his desk and found the spreadsheet for 47. Yes, that was the one. He'd collected almost no information on that connection. The device was confined to a closed room—rudimentary, yet equipped with game consoles and a giant screen—that it wasn't allowed to leave. A teenage boy came in for a few hours at a time to play video games or nap on the sofa. It had been over a month since Grigor connected it, and he still hadn't gotten any details or found a way out of the room.

"What happened?"

"The door was open. I don't know why. So I took the chance to escape."

"And? Do we finally know where we are?'

Grigor picked up a pen, anxious to finally obtain some information. But she signaled him to come closer and sit beside her. She'd taken photos of the tablet screen, a lot of photos, and she wanted to show them to him while she explained.

"You have to see it to understand—this thing is crazy."

Grigor sat down and Nikolina showed him the first images. She'd stored them on the tablet itself, and while she scrolled through the pictures she told him everything, from the beginning. The house turned out to be a humble farm. At first she hadn't seen anyone, and she wanted to find some people and hear what language they spoke, so she went out to the yard. There were untethered dogs that ignored the kentuki, and goats, a lot of loose goats. Nikolina stopped on one photo: he could see an open, flat village in some hot and humid zone, a heavy sky, and not a soul in the photograph, just the road, some houses, goats, and more goats all around.

"You left the house?" asked Grigor, uneasy.

"I know, I know the rules, but wait. Listen first. I couldn't cross the road because it's dirt, see? It wouldn't work."

Grigor looked at the next photo. The place looked like a ghost town, and the goats didn't seem to belong to anyone in particular. There was one lying down in the middle of the street, five more resting in the shade of the awning on an abandoned restaurant, and a larger group farther back, walking away. Amid so much desolation, the sight of a red motorcycle parked in front of one of the houses was alarming; so there *were* people around, thought Grigor.

"But I could move on the sidewalk, see?" Nikolina went on explaining as she skipped to the next photo. "I thought I could check the house next door. But there was no one there, either."

So she'd gone a little farther.

"How far?"

"Two blocks, maybe three."

Grigor clutched his head. It was a stupid risk, going that far from the charger. If someone locked the kentuki up now, if for some reason it couldn't get back to the charger, those weeks of work would be lost.

"Come on, boss," she said finally, interrupting his lecture. "Haven't you ever given in to temptation?"

Plenty of times, but they were *his* kentukis. He knew there was nothing better: to escape from the keepers and move around the connection area autonomously was an extraordinary experience. Extraordinary for *him*, but he wasn't paying this girl to have fun. He looked at her impatiently.

"Wait," she said, "this is important."

Nikolina had entered a house three blocks down, a big, long, one-story house. Her charger had showed 70 percent then, so she thought she had some leeway. Two men were sitting in plastic lawn chairs in the doorway. Nikolina showed him the photo and Grigor saw that, leaning against the wall between the men, there was a shotgun.

"A shotgun?"

Nikolina nodded.

"A shotgun and a lot more goats."

There were so many of them near that house that they helped shield the kentuki from view, and she was able to circle around to the back door. Well, really there was no door, but bars that had been fixed into the threshold.

"Okay, get to the point, you're making me nervous."

One of the dogs, a small one, went inside. It fit easily between the bars, so Nikolina steeled herself and followed it. She showed Grigor the next photo, now inside the house: a dining area open to a rudimentary kitchen, and a woman who was washing dishes, leaning over the sink. Nikolina explained that she crossed the kitchen and went through a door that led to the living room where two more men were talking, slouched on a sofa. She didn't take a photo of that, she went by as fast as she could behind the dog, since she was too exposed and had nowhere to hide.

"What language were they speaking?"

"Portuguese, I think."

Grigor looked at her, impressed and doubtful at the same time.

"You know I love Ronaldinho," said Nikolina, winking at him.

Grigor made a note of the language. Nikolina had followed the dog down the hallway, which led to the bedrooms; there were a lot, some six or seven. The first one had bars on the door, and it was empty. She showed him the photo.

"It's clearly a cell, Grigor. The bed, a blanket, a little table, nothing else."

Grigor made another note, and Nikolina looked at him a moment, disconcerted. She shook her head and went on.

The rest of the rooms were also empty, each with a barred door half-open. There were some images of the beds, which were double and unmade, everything dingy and disheveled.

"In the last room there was a girl," said Nikolina. "The door on that room was closed, but I could fit between the bars, and when the girl saw the kentuki her eyes opened wide. She jumped out of bed like she'd seen a glass of water in the middle of the desert. She ran to the door and laid a chair down so I couldn't get back out again."

"So now we're locked in, without a charger? How many hours now?"

"She's not even fifteen years old, Grigor. She wrote this on a piece of paper and held it in front of the camera."

Nikolina showed him the next photo. It seemed to have been written in lipstick. It was a dirty napkin, and except for the phone number, Grigor was unable to understand what the message said. Nikolina read from her notes:

"'I'm Andrea Farbe, I've been kidnapped. Mom's phone number: +584122340077 please!' It's written in Spanish," clarified Nikolina. "I googled the country code and it's Venezuela. I think we're in Brazil but the girl isn't from there."

Grigor looked at her in horror. She shook her hands as

though she'd burned them, somewhere between frightened and excited.

"We have to get her out. We have to call the mother."

"We don't know where she is."

Grigor explained that the connection system worked on anonymous proxies and jumped automatically from server to server. Even if there was a way to pinpoint the kentuki's location, the only thing they would get in a period of searching would be expired signals from almost everywhere in the world. Nikolina put her hand over her mouth. They sat for a moment and thought.

Grigor picked up tablet 47 and saw the girl for the first time, not in photos, but live. Skinny, with dark circles under her eyes, she was desperately searching through drawers, and she seemed to be taking care not to make any noise. The walls were concrete and the black-and-pink sheets looked to be made of cheap, synthetic material.

"We need a charger," said Grigor. "If we stay here with her, we might be able to figure out where we are, but who knows how long that could take. In the meantime, we need battery power."

"Hold on, she's writing on the floor now," said Nikolina. "Turn the kentuki around."

He turned it. The girl had drawn a cross on the floor in lipstick, and now she was writing in the four rectangles. She wrote NO in the upper left, SI in the upper right, NO SE in the bottom left, and in the last one: PREGUNTA MAS. Nikolina was looking up each word in a translator.

"Confirmed," she said, "it's Spanish.

"This is no good," said Grigor. "We're the ones who need

to be asking questions, we'll never figure out where she is this way."

A notification warned them that the battery had hit 50 percent. Nikolina took the tablet from Grigor and moved the kentuki over the rectangle for PREGUNTA MAS, maybe because out of the four options, *Ask more* was the closest thing to *Tell us more*.

The girl spoke, but they didn't understand.

NO, Nikolina had the kentuki say, PREGUNTA MAS.

The girl cursed under her breath and looked to either side, desperately shaking her head.

Nikolina went over to the lipstick and pushed it toward the girl's feet.

"Where are you?!" she shouted at the tablet, while behind her Grigor twisted himself up in his chair, trying to think of something.

A little later, when the battery was already down to 30 percent, the girl seemed to calm down and think things out better. She wrote something on the other side of the napkin and showed it to them:

Surumu.

Grigor looked at Nikolina.

"So what's she speaking now?"

Nikolina googled it. She ruled out some of the results and then cried out:

"It's a place! Surumu is a village in the state of Roraima, it's in Brazil."

She found it right away, only a few miles from the border with Venezuela. It was such a small town it didn't even have its own Wikipedia page. Nikolina put the photo of the napkin with the phone number on it in front of Grigor, and he dialed it. As he did he was trembling and silently cursing his luck, wondering if he would have made that call if Nikolina hadn't been there to pressure him. He asked in English if he was speaking with the mother of Andrea Farbe, and the woman who answered was silent for a few seconds and then burst out crying. Nikolina took the phone and tried to soothe her. She quickly realized the woman didn't understand a word of English, and that she was crying because she'd heard her daughter's name. So Nikolina hung up and called the closest police station to Surumu they could find, 317 kilometers away. They were passed along from one extension to another, transferred as soon as the person realized they weren't speaking Portuguese, until finally someone with a basic command of English answered. They tried to explain what was happening, but every time the cop seemed to finally understand, the connection went dead. Nikolina called back; it took several tries before she understood what had been clear to Grigor from the start—the local police were most likely involved in whatever was going on in Surumu.

Nikolina called other nearby police stations. Either they hung up on her, too, or they refused to speak English, or they kept her waiting endlessly on the phone. Grigor thought it would be enough to take a picture of the girl's image and get in touch with some media outlet to get things really moving, although he wondered if that wouldn't be a reckless move. What Grigor hadn't realized—but deduced when Nikolina suggested a similar solution—was that she'd been recording the calls to all the police stations, and had eight different conversations saved on her phone. Nikolina called several outlets in both Venezuela and Brazil and handed over all the material.

Some hours later Grigor's phone rang; it was the Venezuelan police. The Brazilian federal police also called, and the headquarters of the general police department of Roraima. In Surumu, the girl had asked if they'd made the call, holding her hand up to her. Nikolina had indicated SI, and the girl had been crying silently since. Grigor enumerated for Nikolina the possible consequences of what they had just done, and then the two of them were silent for a while, perhaps each taking stock of how far they were willing to go for this stranger in peril.

"We have to move everything," said Nikolina finally, and it wasn't until she gathered up her personal belongings along with the first two tablet boxes and went out into the hallway that Grigor understood what she meant.

They moved all sixty-two of their functioning tablets to her small apartment across the hall. They took apart the table Nikolina used as a desk and moved it back to the kitchen. They hid the spreadsheets and the cameras with their tripods. They carried away anything that could incriminate them. When the Croatian police knocked on Grigor's apartment door there was only one tablet left, and it wasn't kentuki number 47's. Grigor didn't trust the police, and he'd decided it was better to maintain the connection and follow what was happening in Surumu as long as possible. So he sacrificed a kentuki he would have gotten very little for anyway: he ended the connection, and apologetically gave the cleared tablet to the police instead of number 47.

Meanwhile, the real 47 was agonizing on another continent, down to its last 10 percent of battery. They turned back to that problem as soon as the police were gone.

"We have to get it to the charger."

"No," said Nikolina. "We can't leave the girl. Not at a time like this."

"If we stay here," said Grigor, "we won't last much more than fifteen minutes. If we move, a miracle could still happen."

Nikolina nodded. They guided the kentuki over to the chair and tapped against it a few times. The girl understood and removed it. The dog was sitting in the middle of the hallway waiting for them, and it sniffed at them again as they headed toward the kitchen. There was only one man on the sofa now, and he was asleep. The radio was on. Nikolina left the house, and, skirting some potholes of concrete and dirt, pausing between the goats' feet and making sure they didn't kick her over, she guided the kentuki along the sidewalk of that ghost town, now dark and nocturnal. It was a wonder to watch her control the kentuki; Grigor had never seen her work from so close up, and he was impressed. She was a virtuoso. Back at the other house, the goats were still outside and the doors open, same as in the morning. When Nikolina finally fit the kentuki on the charger, they both shouted and high-fived. They had power.

Oaxaca

• •

ALINA SAT DOWN on the steps near the fountains and took off her sneakers so the heat from the flagstones would dry her damp feet. She thought of Carmen, who claimed that artists always smelled bad, especially their feet. They were beautiful as the gods of Olympus—"hot and crazy," as Carmen said peevishly—but they smelled like hell itself, and every time one of them came in for a book, Carmen had to air out the whole library. Did she smell as bad as the artists after she ran ten kilometers? She was sitting on the top steps of the embankment. On the other side of the fountains, a kentuki—not the Colonel—rolled along in the shade of the exhibition hall and headed off toward the gallery.

Now there were kentukis everywhere. Alina had counted five at the residency. A few days ago, the crazy woman with the cork installations had taken a mole kentuki that wasn't hers from the kitchen, and the Russian, who had the same color mole, had taken hers. Sven told her about it in full detail. Neither of the artists had realized the mix-up. Not until the dweller of the Russian's mole—that is, the dweller of the kentuki now in the possession of the crazy cork lady—sent an audio message to his keeper's phone. It was the first time the Russian had heard that voice, and he didn't know who it was or what language it was speaking. He played it at dinner and one of the Chilean photographers said it sounded like Welsh—her mother was Welsh, and she recognized it right away. So the Russian forwarded it to the Chilean woman and the Chilean sent it to her mother, who translated it and recorded the same message but in Spanish, which the Chilean was kind enough to repeat in English for everyone, trying to maintain her mother's intonation. The message said: "Either get me away from this crazy lady, or I'm disconnecting!" The cork artist was among the curious listeners who had gathered to hear the translated message. It took her a few seconds to realize it was referring to her; then, furious, she grabbed her kentuki—that is, the Russian's kentuki, and she stomped on it as hard as she could. The first kick only knocked it over on the floor—the Russian leapt to try and save it—but with the second stomp, her high heel drove directly into the camera eye and crushed in the creature's face, laying bare the metal. The rest of the artists pulled her away and tried to soothe her. In the commotion the other mole disappeared, and no one saw it again. The beaten kentuki had survived, it was shrieking, and the Russian carried it away in his arms, soothing it with what to Sven was the most chilling lullaby he'd heard in his life.

Things like that were all Sven talked about those days. Artists and their kentukis. Alina just listened.

She went to her room and showered. Then, sitting at the

desk, she stretched in her chair, pulled her hair up into a big bun, and checked the savings in her bank account. She wanted to go back to Mendoza early, even though she was short on cash.

Are you sure you're ok? her mother kept asking by text.

She sent emojis of faces blowing kisses, of watermelons and cats, and she attached photos of Alina's nieces.

Alina replied that she was fine, and sent little skull emojis.

Carmen had promised that the Day of the Dead would be the best thing to happen in Alina's whole visit. She wouldn't let her leave before she saw how good the Oaxacans were at celebrating. By now, Carmen and Alina were having coffee at the kiosk every afternoon. Alina suggested that they go down together to Oaxaca on the night of the Day of the Dead. It would be fun, they could go from bar to bar and stay out until morning. For a moment Carmen smiled. The plan was a good one, but Alina was forgetting that Carmen, aside from being a librarian, was a mother of two boys—two boys with kentukis.

"It'll be a sleepless night for me in any case."

"Sleepless?" asked Alina.

"It's just kids' nonsense," said Carmen, "this thing about the kentuki boycott. They want to spend the night hugging their kitties to be sure nothing happens to them. They want to nail boards up over the windows and turn the lights off inside, like it's a damned zombie attack."

Carmen finished her coffee in one long sip and sat looking at the mountains.

"And their father," she said, "instead of calming them down, bought them each an emergency backpack with flashlights, sleeping bags, red paint guns . . . You get the idea of what's in store for me."

As soon as Alina got back to the room, she turned on her tablet and googled *boycott, kentukis, day of the dead.* The Colonel would be about to come back from the studios and knock on the door, but what she'd just heard now had her full attention. Apparently, the movement had been born in Las Brisas, a neighborhood in Acapulco with narrow streets full of palm trees and designer houses, one of the twenty neighborhoods in the world where, according to the *Financial Times,* one out of every four families had at least one kentuki in the house. The surveys showed some nine losses a week, and in a small neighborhood like that one, where people had enough money to replace them immediately, it was starting to become a problem. The yards were too small to be burying pets, and people didn't want to throw their kentukis in the garbage. Nearby, in the Unta Bruja area, a mother with two disconsolate children had gone to a shady corner—the closest thing to a public space to be found for miles—and dug a kind of grave, where they'd held funerals for two panda kentukis. Some days later, more graves appeared around the first. The space couldn't hold many more bodies, and even so, there were more burial grounds appearing here and there in Las Brisas, in the few little public plazas that existed, and extending into other neighborhoods along Avenida Miguel Alemán.

The municipal council had ordered the parks department to remove the graves and repair the damage to public property. The next day, an elderly couple stationed themselves in front of city hall to reclaim the body of their kentuki. On social media people were indignant, but no one buried kentukis in public places after that. A rock-star sociologist on TV called for a massive burial in every state in Mexico on the night of the Day of the Dead. His brother—an anti-imperialist reggaeton artist and standard-bearer for a nascent political party that was hot on the government's heels—had ended his last concert with a disquieting counterproposal, yelling into the microphone: "Don't bury the dead, bury live kentukis!" which had generated a confused discussion in the media. In the end, predictably, the mood had calmed down and the revolutionary boycott had been lost amid much more alarming and real political noise. The disquiet remained only among the youngest, where concerns were soon assuaged with a jump in sales of all kinds of survival-related accessories marketed to children who owned kentukis.

When Colonel Sanders tapped at the door, Alina bookmarked the article she was reading and got up to let him in; he looked strange without his little wings. He had a clod of dirt stuck in one of his wheels and it turned with difficulty. Alina didn't say anything, and she let him roll off toward his charger. The base was still beside the bed, though some days ago Sven had moved it to his side. He'd done it while she was asleep. Alina took off her sandals and flopped on the bed. For a week now, before she lay her head on the pillow, she'd been checking underneath it to be sure Sven hadn't put anything there. She missed his big, square hands, and she kept thinking that, why not, he could also have left something for her. Tangerine peels or any other kind of signal, maybe something so minuscule she couldn't even detect it. Then she lay down and stared at the ceiling.

What was it she'd been waiting for, so many days and weeks just sitting around on the double bed? Something unprecedented from Sven? Something unprecedented from herself? And the kentukis . . . That was what most infuriated her. What was the whole stupid idea of the kentukis about? What were all those people doing rolling around on other people's floors, watching how the other half of humanity brushed their teeth? Why didn't anyone collude with kentukis to hatch truly brutal plots? Why didn't anyone send a kentuki loaded with explosives into a crowded central station and blow it all to smithereens? Why didn't any kentuki user blackmail an air traffic controller and force him to immolate five planes in Frankfurt in exchange for his daughter's life? Why didn't even one single user out of the thousands who must be moving at that very moment over truly important papers take note of some crucial detail and break the Wall Street markets, or hack into some software network and make all the elevators fall simultaneously in a dozen skyscrapers? Why wasn't there a single miserable morning when thousands of consumers woke up dead from a simple bucket of lithium poured into a Brazilian milk factory? Why were the stories about kentukis so small, so minutely intimate, stingy, and predictable? So desperately human and quotidian. Not even the boycott on the Day of the Dead would bear results, she was sure. And Sven would never change his art for her. Nor would she change, for anyone, her state of existential fragmentation. Everything faded.

She would buy her tickets to go back home for the first days of November, decided Alina. That way she could attend, unnoticed, Sven's blessed exhibition that people were talking about so much in the residency's hallways, and then, a day or two later, she'd get on a plane and hide away in dear old Mendoza forever. She'd take the kentuki with her. On the flight, she thought, she would put it in an upper compartment of the cabin and then never take it off the plane. Leave it there. Let someone else's tits be randomly assigned to the Colonel.

Antigua — Honningsvåg

• •

THERE WAS A LOT TO TELL. At school he gave a report to his friends during the first break every day, and there were more and more kids who wanted to listen. There were four kentuki keepers in his class and a lot more who dwelled in kentukis, and some were on their second or even third life. But none of them lived in the land of Vikings, much less moved around liberated with a map of charger bases. Marvin's situation was the best that people could get in their kentuki life. Restricted as he was to a schedule between eleven at night and two in the morning in Norway, he encountered very few people, and a lot of those he did come across were drunk—which never stopped being funny. Plus, if you were the height of a kentuki, you could see things around town that no one else did. The Liberation Club was everywhere: there was graffiti on the curbs and at the bottoms of the walls of houses. Arrows pointing you toward overhanging roofs in case it rained, dozens of homes willing to offer small repairs and chargers.

The day before, at the base of a park bench, he read:

All the best to you, SnowDragon! Write us!

He thought about Kitty03, and wondered how much she'd paid Jesper to paint those words. It was silly to be there, alone in the middle of the night, when he had so many friends on the other side of town who were just waiting for a word from him. Reaching the snow was taking him a lot longer than he'd calculated, but he wasn't going back until he'd done it. He opened the map and studied his options for a while.

It was while he was distracted with the map that someone lifted him from the ground. He was on a dark corner and he hadn't seen a soul, and all of a sudden there were two boys throwing him around. Where had they come from? They looked like brothers and they must have been around Marvin's age, maybe a little younger. They were carrying slingshots. The smaller one had picked him up, and the older one snatched him away and tugged on his wheels as if trying to pull them off. His dragon fell to the ground and rolled, and the boys picked it back up. He couldn't move fast enough. They shouted and fought over him, and the camera shook so much that he could barely figure out what was happening. In the struggle he saw part of the harness Jesper had used to attach the second battery lying on the ground. Marvin was scared. They pulled on him and threw him again. The younger boy cried out when his brother tried to take the kentuki away. Marvin didn't think twice, and activated the alarm. How long would it take Jesper to get there? He remembered that the alarm, in addition to activating the locator, should have left everyone around him deaf, but there was no sound. The dragon fell and rolled again. Marvin went on activating the alarm. It wasn't working. He rolled up against the curb and miraculously managed to stand up on his wheels again. He tried to move away. A dog ran up to him and barked, baring its teeth. The boys came up behind him and lifted him up again. There was a man with the dog, and now he was in the man's hands. The boys yelled in annoyance and the man scolded them, shoved them toward a truck and opened the cabin door for them. They got in, pulling each other's hair. The man left the kentuki in back, in the truck bed. Marvin moved as soon as the man let go of him, though there was really nowhere to go. The metal of the bed was rusty, and there was no wall or railing on the sides, just a trench that barely marked the edges. Boxes of apples were piled up in the middle, secured to the cabin with cables. The man rummaged around to open the plastic covering on the first box, took out three apples, and left. He got into the truck and shook it with a slam of his door. The motor started up and the image on Marvin's screen shook. He tried to find something to hold on to, finally pressing his face into the boxes. The town moved, they were passing houses and shops as they started off through Honningsvåg in the opposite direction from the snow. The truck turned, and Marvin had to make a great effort not to lose his balance. He thought about letting himself topple off, but the landscape was speeding by too fast; he wasn't sure he would survive such a fall. Soon the town was left behind and they got onto the highway, moving uphill and away from the sea.

He thought that if they didn't go much farther and he paid enough attention, it would still be possible to find his way back. Soon there was no trace of the town left. The road dipped back down and a lake opened up at the bottom of the slope. A dock and two humble shacks went racing by. Beyond the lake, climbing up the hillside, he saw the snow. He was far away, but he was going toward it. They went straight for a good while. It was whiter than he had ever imagined.

"Marvin!" His father's voice came from the dining room, calling him to dinner.

The truck left the highway and took a dirt road, and the camera's jolting kept him from seeing clearly. He was afraid an especially hard bump would dump a box of apples on top of him, but there was nothing Marvin could do. A rough bounce threw the kentuki into the air. Marvin was sure he would fall out of the truck. He hit against the metal with his wheels and was able to maneuver quickly back to the center of the bed, as close as possible to the boxes. The image on his tablet was growing darker. Now all he could see was the truck's red lights shining on the moving asphalt and, far away, almost in the sky, the snow lit up by the moon.

His father called him again, this time from the stairs, closer.

The truck sped up—it was going too fast. There was another bump, and it finally made him lose his balance. He rolled to the back, hit against the metal of the cabin and rolled forward again. They took another exit; it was steep, and some apples hit the camera. Everything was still shaking. It was impossible to stand up, impossible to brake against anything. He rolled up to one of the edges, and the groove in the metal held him in for a moment, but one final bump sent him flying into the air again.

He fell. He felt the emptiness under his wheels, the blow against the asphalt, the screech of his rubber and his plastic and his metal rolling pell-mell down the hill.

His father's voice yelled his name from the other side of the door, and Marvin had to make an effort not to burst out crying. He was rolling, he was still rolling toward the lake when he thought of his mother and the snow. It seemed that he was to have nothing, that God would insist on taking away the things that mattered most. He was still rolling when his father opened the door. Marvin moved the tablet and set it on his books, gritted his teeth so hard he thought he wouldn't be able to move any other part of his body. The noise from the fall could still be heard, metallic, emanating from the tablet into the room. What would he do if his father asked what was going on? How would he explain that in reality he was beaten up, he was broken, and he was still rolling, out of control, down a hill? He made an effort and managed to breathe. Could his father hear him falling? Did he understand that the noise on the tablet came from Marvin's own body hitting the gravel? He looked at his father, who, with a movement of his head, told him to come. Marvin got down from the chair. When he passed his father he saw the school report card hanging from his hand. It was as if Marvin couldn't feel the ground, as if he were walking on air. He reached the stairs, and before he started down them, he stopped. The whole house felt too light, unreal. It took him a second to recognize the silence, to accept that it came from the tablet.

"Down," his father said.

Marvin wanted to tell him it was impossible, that he felt sick and dizzy, that he couldn't go down any farther than he already had. He heard his father close the door to the study, and then the sound of the key and footsteps behind him.

Marvin had to lean against the marble handrail. For a moment, the cold stung the tips of his fingers. He thought of his mother. It was only a few seconds, and then the Antigua heat pulled him out of it.

"Down," he heard again.

His father's hand was pushing on his back. Step after step, farther and farther down.

Zagreb — Surumu

· ·

AT NOON, TWO DIFFERENT DELIVERYMEN took away tablets to fill five late orders. Plan Fallback had reached a point where, even with Nikolina's help and after almost quadrupling his prices, he was selling more units than they were able to replace. But Grigor knew the cycles of boom businesses. Prices were already going down and clearance sales were multiplying by the day. Resellers always saw their prices fall last, and soon he would feel the decline, too.

The Surumu madness had kept Nikolina in Grigor's room for two nights and three days. Glued to the news and the phone, which still sometimes rang, they'd largely ignored the other kentukis, and now they had a lot of work to catch up on. They slept in shifts and ate basically nothing but crackers and the yogurt Grigor's father still brought them on schedule, oblivious to all that was happening.

The Surumu kentuki was still in a torturous limbo. When the five-hour charge was complete, Nikolina woke the device and saw with relief that the doors to the house were still open.

In Zagreb, she shook Grigor, who was sleeping on the floor at her feet, and together they went back out to the sidewalk to evaluate their surroundings. They were crossing the second block when someone picked them up. They saw the sky, still gray and lowering. They saw—Nikolina was convinced—two police cars on the sidewalk across the street, their lights on. Then there was only darkness, as if they'd been put in a bag or their camera had been blindfolded. There didn't seem to be anything beneath their wheels.

"We're in the air," said Grigor. "We'd better save power."

They deduced from the sound that they'd been put into a truck, or maybe some kind of trailer. Though they were on the floor, there was nowhere to move. Maybe they'd been put in a box or the trunk of a car. Nikolina stopped all actions on the controller and left the tablet on the table in *Sleep* mode.

Since then they had opened the kentuki's eyes from time to time to check on what was happening, and every time they were greeted by that devastating blackness. No one spoke, they didn't hear anything. They tried to find news online, but there was only some vague civil indignation over the recordings that they themselves had handed over to the media; there was no official information. So they went to work on the other connections they were behind schedule on.

They tried to distract themselves with other tablets, but deep down all their attention was on that suspended connection in Brazil. They worked, dozed in shifts on the bed, and then went back to work. When fifteen hours had passed since what Nikolina referred to as "the kidnapping," she woke the

kentuki, and, though she was still in the dark, she heard voices
and doors and there were some halos of light, as if she were
moving in an open space. Grigor came right over. He shook
his head, disconcerted.

What the hell is happening? he thought.

"Should I make noise?" asked Nikolina.

"Let's wait, wait till we see something."

They spent almost another day in darkness. Nikolina turned
on the kentuki ever more sporadically to preserve the charge,
until they connected on the fifth day and found the situation
had completely changed.

They were in a dining room; it was large, but the house
was humble. The walls were old and unpainted, there were
two plastic tables to one side, and a screen divided the rest of
the room. Three big windows without curtains opened onto
an outer gallery, and beyond that, there was jungle. They were
in a tropical zone. Three children were playing on the floor
and they looked curiously at the kentuki, maybe because it
was the first time they'd seen it move. One of them got up
and went running to a room on the left, returning with two
women in tow.

"It's her!" cried Nikolina.

When the girl saw the kentuki awake, she greeted it with
emotion. The woman behind her seemed to be her mother,
and she looked on curiously, drying her hands on her apron.
They came closer. The girl had a piece of chalk and she drew
on the floor in front of the kentuki, reproducing the simple
cross they had tried to communicate with before. Mother
and daughter looked at the camera and spoke to them joy-

fully, interrupting each other. They seemed to be thanking them, though neither Grigor nor Nikolina could make out a word, and again, the girl's cross only offered answers to questions. They couldn't think of a way to say they weren't understanding a thing.

"They seem like very good people." Nikolina was clearly moved to see them again, too.

Grigor gave her a gentle pat on her shoulder, and she looked at him in surprise. They spent a while with the kentuki, interacting as best they could with the girl and her mother, the curious children in the background. Then the mother waved goodbye and left. Nikolina looked for the mother's number and called her again, thinking she could suggest to the girl some other method of communication. The phone rang in the house and the girl went to answer. Grigor would have preferred not to keep getting involved, but it was too late, she had already answered.

"It's us," said Nikolina, in English. "Are you all right?"

She repeated the question in English and then in a pretty basic French that Grigor had never heard from her. It was clear the girl didn't understand either. What kind of community was this where everyone seemed to be up-to-date on what a kentuki was, but no one spoke a word of English? Grigor thought the girl hadn't even managed to connect the kentuki to the phone call she'd just received. She hung up and said something to the kids, who laughed.

Nikolina put down the tablet. She seemed disappointed, but she also looked like someone who'd had a great weight taken off her shoulders.

"Now I really need a good shower," she said. She stretched, reaching her octopus arms upward. She stood up and went to the door. "Thank you," she said from the doorway to the room, before leaving, and she smiled.

Grigor smiled back. He felt a little dumb when the girl was gone and the grin still stretched across his face. Alone in the room, he thought for a while about those long and flexible arms, the alien vertebrae covered in velvety skin. Maybe, even after all that had happened with connection 47, he hadn't lost so much. He grabbed the tablet, sat on the bed, and maneuvered the kentuki for a while around the girl's house, evaluating the socioeconomic conditions of the environment. If he was lucky, in spite of all it had been through, he could still sell that kentuki. In the end the connection was linked to a criminal case, and more than once people had written to ask about even more morbid kinds of connections. So this one was worth some money. Plus, the house was a humble place, almost at the edge of acceptable, but the landscape was pleasant and the family seemed quaint, and there were always upper-class Europeans who wanted to circulate their philanthropic instincts around areas of the world too uncomfortable to be visited in the traditional ways. The girl and her mother seemed like good people, it had to be said, and the kids were obedient and respectful: they followed him curiously, but they didn't get too close or touch him. The girl walked away and Grigor followed her. They went into the kitchen, also large and also unfinished. Two men were talking at the table while the mother did dishes at the sink. The girl exchanged a few words with her; they looked happy, uninterested in the conversation between the two men. When Grigor got closer to them, he thought he understood why: they were speaking English. The older man—surely the father—seemed to speak it haltingly.

"I . . . No money, no money. Already spent."

The other man was younger. His skin was white and he was smoking. His pronunciation was almost perfect.

"Your girl is back, man. Don't you get it? If the girl came home, the money goes back into the Don's wallet."

The girl came over with two plates and set one in front of each man. The younger one took her by the wrist and kissed her arm, looking at the father. Then, without letting go of her, he said:

"They're not asking."

She didn't seem to have the slightest idea what they were talking about, but her smile suddenly disappeared, as if she'd been hit by a still incomprehensible revelation.

Grigor imagined himself to be as invisible as his kentuki there beside the cupboards, and he stayed where he was for a moment, listening to the mother call to the girl. He thought about Nikolina, and whether he would be capable of telling her what they had really returned the girl to. He thought about his own father, his yogurt, and the money he had finally managed to save up thanks to Plan Fallback. And then he had a realization: he didn't want to keep watching strangers eat and snore, he never wanted to see a single chick shrieking in terror while the rest plucked its feathers in panic, he didn't want to move anyone else from one inferno to another. He wasn't going to wait until the damned international regulations came to remove him from the business—they'd already taken too long. He was getting out by himself. He'd sell the connections he had left, and he'd start doing something else. He went to the general settings, and without even bothering to get the kentuki out of that house first, he cut the connection.

Lima—Erfurt

· ·

SHE'D DREAMED ABOUT KLAUS. She had moved in bed, between the sheets, and she'd felt him embrace her in the darkness. And then, something worse. Something hot and wet,
and a large, stiff German member between her legs jolted her
awake. She was so alarmed she had to sit up for a moment
and turn on the bedside lamp. Then she saw her bunny. It
was in the middle of the room, its open eyes looking at her
sweetly. Had it seen her dreaming? Could it have seen more
than it should have? They'd been living together for almost a
week now, a week so harmonious and full of love that Emilia
would have been ashamed to admit it. Except to Gloria. She'd
told Gloria because she was her great friend in this adventure, and they could trust each other. To her son, on the
other hand, she'd said nothing. He was too fascinated with
the woman and her black boots, too busy lately to answer his
mother with the slightest bit of interest, and when it came
to kentukis, he was more interested in talking than in listening.

What worried Emilia was how little the boy watched out

for his privacy: she was indignant that even she, who was from another generation and had spent a whole life far removed from technology, was so much more aware of the exposure and risk implied by a relationship with those critters. She saw it every day on the news. They invited specialists on the ten p.m. show who listed new tips and precautions like they were giving the weather report. Emilia thought it was a matter of common sense, and of knowing how to set limits. You only had to have life experience and a little intuition. But it was worth taking the risk, because at the end of the day there were little creatures like hers, and like the one she was in Erfurt. Beings with good intentions who only wanted to share their time with others.

That's how it had been with Eva at first. Klaus had brought problems, but now the days were flowing calmly again. Although the German still called her. The first few times Emilia saw his number glowing on the screen she trembled. She paced back and forth holding the phone, unsure what to do. In the end she always answered. The German spoke to her in thickly accented, largely unintelligible English, and a lot of what he said escaped her. Still, by the third or fourth call, she started to feel a familiarity with that deep voice, and she realized it wasn't really all that important to decipher what he said. She suspected, with all the open-mindedness of which she'd turned out to be capable in these past months, that maybe there was something more behind the lasciviousness and aggression of those calls. She told herself it was necessary to make the effort to listen to him, that it was an opportunity to find out more details of the girl's world. She did it for Eva, for the two of them—Emilia and Eva. She listened to the

German's voice and closed her eyes, trying to understand. Sometimes Klaus's tone implied a question and then he'd fall silent, and then Emilia would say some silly thing in Spanish, about the weather or the news of the day, until Klaus interrupted and started to talk again. He was always the one to hang up. Emilia, of course, stuck it out until the end.

She pushed the sheets aside, put on her dressing gown, and got up. The bunny followed her to the kitchen and they put on water for tea. It hadn't even been a week and they already had their routine. At first Emilia had tried to resist the bunny's charms. She thought that seeing such a true reflection of herself—of the animal she was in Erfurt—moving around all day at her feet could be treacherous, could make her trust more than she should. But the respect she felt from the kentuki was remarkable. It was just that the similarity didn't come only from the silly appearance of being two bunnies with the same color fur, the same barrette placed between their ears in the same way. It was like constantly seeing herself; they seemed like kindred spirits in almost every way possible, and sometimes it even pained her to leave the kentuki locked in the house when she went to the store.

Soon she began to tell it things. She thought back over the questions she'd always wanted to ask Eva and she answered them for her bunny, in case she was wondering the same things: how her keeper had come to live in that house, the most important points of her family history, what people in the neighborhood were like, and who she should vote for if she lived in that city.

"You're the only person I know who's a keeper and a dweller at the same time," Gloria had told her.

They talked about kentukis in secret, in the showers at the pool while Inés was swimming her final laps.

"That must give you a special perspective, right?"

It was possible, yes, she did realize that. Sometimes she moved around the apartment in Erfurt looking for Eva, while she heard her own bunny moving behind her like a deferred echo of herself. And for her bunny it must be soothing to watch its keeper dwell in a kentuki. It made you think about all the branches of understanding and solidarity such an exercise implied. But what had she become? Some kind of Zen monk of the bifurcated meanings of kentukis? Well, she was someone who was learning a lot, she couldn't deny that.

"They understand everything, you know," she said to the man at the supermarket later, reprimanding him.

She was paying at the register and saw that the cashier had his kentuki on the counter, moving over the invoices and receipts. She didn't think it was smart to give it so much freedom around people's financial information, and Emilia was starting to suspect that, if there were abuses by some kentukis, it was only because of their keepers' negligence. Boundaries were really the very foundation of these relationships. At the end of the day, that was how she had raised her son, and he hadn't turned out half bad.

Back home after the supermarket she stored the food in the fridge and made lunch. Every time she opened and closed the refrigerator door, she saw the image she'd printed out of her and Eva in Erfurt. She'd printed other photos as well while she was at it, images she took of her computer screen with her phone, and she'd hung them up here and there, and even put one in a very pretty frame her son had given her. She had also printed some of Klaus. She liked the ones of the German cooking in his underwear. For now—except for the two on her bathroom mirror—those were on the nightstand. And there was a very funny one Emilia wanted to use to make a card for Gloria. Deep down, she had to admit, she wanted her friend to see what kind of man it was who called her some afternoons.

Emilia watched the news while she ate lunch, and then she cleaned the kitchen. She used those hours for household chores because it was a time when her bunny tended to sleep. She left it on its charger, as Eva did with her. When she lifted it up, she always checked anxiously to make sure the discreet little light between the back wheels was on. Gloria had explained that was the only way of making sure that, even if the little creature was asleep, it was still connected.

At two in the afternoon, nice and punctual, they were in front of the computer, waking up in Erfurt. Sometimes the bunny asked to get up, too, and Emilia set her in front of the screen. It must have been fascinating for her to see herself in another place, controlled by her keeper.

"It's Erfurt, Germany." Emilia passed on details to help orient her new friend.

The bunny purred, touched her arms, looked into her eyes, and blinked. She liked Erfurt, but clearly didn't like Klaus. The last time he'd called, the kentuki had looked at the number lighting up the phone screen, motionless as if the devil himself were calling. Maybe she noticed her keeper's tension. Maybe she even understood something of what Klaus was saying into Emilia's ear, and didn't like it.

"It's nothing bad, little one," Emilia said after she hung up. "Don't you worry."

On the Erfurt screen, Klaus had left the phone on the kitchen table and was making a sandwich. He went back and forth in his underwear, opening the fridge, breaking some eggs into a pan, almost without ever putting down his beer. Emilia wondered if he said the same words to Eva when they were in bed together as he said to her, and the shame made her glance at her bunny out of the corner of her eye. Then Klaus's phone rang, in Erfurt. Klaus lowered the flame and answered. Emilia liked his German much more than his English, though she didn't understand in the slightest and his tone was so different from the one he used with her. Klaus was listening, serious. He went over to the window with his head bent over the phone; he seemed to be paying close attention to what someone was saying. Emilia had no idea what it was all about, but he was unusually attentive—this was a strange call.

Suddenly, Klaus looked over at her. He stared at Emilia in a way that alarmed her, like that first time just before he'd chased her down like a chicken. Klaus came over to her, nodding into the phone. Just then Eva opened the door to the apartment and came in. She was returning from yoga, her mat and bag slung over her shoulder. Klaus covered the mouthpiece on his phone and explained something to her, and then Eva also looked at Emilia, still holding her things, as if she was trying to comprehend the news she'd just received. The two of them stared at Emilia, and Emilia stared at them on the screen. She couldn't figure out what was happening. Klaus turned his attention back to the phone and nodded. He wrote something on a piece of paper and said a few words before hanging up. Then he went over to Eva, showing her his screen, running his finger across it as if showing her several images. Eva looked. Her mouth was in a strange grimace, and then a smile escaped her; it was a brief and perverse expression Emilia had never seen her make before. Eva dropped her bag and yoga mat and sat down. She looked at the kentuki on the floor, and Emilia moved closer to her feet because she wanted to see her up close, so desperate was she to understand what was happening. Eva knelt down next to her. She sat on the floor with her legs crossed and the phone in her hand, and dialed.

The phone in Emilia's house rang. Too many things were happening for her to answer. The device vibrated on the desk until her bunny pushed it over to her and left it against her hand. It was Klaus's number. When Emilia answered, Eva looked at her and smiled. She spoke in German, but the translator was still working on the screen.

"Hello."

Eva's voice sounded harder and more adult over the phone.

"Your little bunny just sent me photos of you chatting on the phone with my boyfriend. Photos of your house full of pictures of us. Also photos of you. I think you've got your puritan little bunny all in a tizzy."

Emilia wanted to understand, but she couldn't understand.

"Your little bunny seems very disappointed in its keeper. And I want to tell you something . . ." Eva's voice became deeper and slower, so sensual it made the hair stand up on the back of Emilia's neck. *"Emilia . . ."* Eva knew her name. *"I really, really like your old-lady underwear."*

She'd been seen in her beige underpants? The ones that came up nearly to the bottom of her breasts?

"A lot," said Eva, looking at Klaus. *"We both do."*

Emilia jumped in the chair and spilled the tea that was beside her. She stood up without knowing what to do, her heart pounding dangerously fast. She realized she was still holding the phone to her ear.

"Miss . . ." she tried to say, and her weak and scratchy voice reminded her how old she was.

She didn't know how to go on. She hung up. In Erfurt, Eva looked at the phone and said something inaudible to Klaus, who burst out laughing, took Eva by the arm, pulled her to her feet, and started to take off her yoga pants. Emilia turned off the screen, furious. Then she turned it back on and Eva was pulling down Klaus's underpants. How did this nightmare disconnect? She fumbled for the controller and found the red button she'd ignored so many times before.

Annul connection?

Emilia accepted and kept her hands glued to the chair's backrest. She squeezed the chair until it made noise, leaving a permanent mark. A red warning came on-screen: **Connection ended.** It was the first time Emilia had seen something so big and red on her computer, but her body didn't seem capable of responding to any new stimulus. She was motionless, exhausted from so much fright and abuse. The kentuki looked at her from the other end of the desk, seeming to judge her, and Emilia wasn't willing to put up with its disapproval. She had a sudden memory of Klaus: he had taught her exactly how chickens were killed in the modern world. Emilia picked up the rabbit, brought it to the kitchen, and set it in the sink.

When she let go of it to turn on the faucet, the kentuki tried to get away, but she took it roughly by the ears, with all the rage and frustration she was capable of, and she held it under the stream of water. The rabbit screeched and shook, and Emilia wondered what her son would think if he could see her at that moment, how ashamed he would be if he could see her viselike hands holding the rabbit under the water, covering its little eyes and pressing it against the drain with all her strength, drowning it, until the little green light on its base stopped blinking.

Umbertide

· ·

IT HAD BEEN almost two weeks since he'd seen Luca. At some point during all the meetings with the psychologist, the arguments with his ex-wife, and the social worker's intervention, Enzo had started to face up to the idea that he might actually lose custody of his son.

He was ashamed when he remembered that, only two years before, a judge had concluded that his wife wasn't stable enough to take responsibility for the boy, and he was terrified that same judge would think he'd now become an even worse option. He knew the psychologist had spent hours and hours talking with Luca, and he supposed that, better educated and better informed than his ex-wife about all the world's perversions, the doctor must have listed them for Luca over and over, lubricating details if she thought something wasn't understood well enough, or drawing the unnameable on paper if the boy's replies were ambiguous. But Enzo could no longer protect him, and it was his own fault. They would tell him everything, ask him anything, and the boy would have to learn to live with it.

The "evaluation of damages" took three sessions in one week and a visit to the police station, all four of them: a father, two crazy ladies, and a boy. Or three adults and a boy; or a boy who never should have had to go to a police station and who deserved someone better than any one of those three adults. Luca bore it all in silence. The lawsuit against the kentuki that the women demanded. The legal impossibility of such a suit that the official in charge tried to explain to them numerous times. Enzo had to sign a mutual-agreement contract in which he pledged to disconnect the kentuki, agreed to move immediately into a new house with a new phone number, and accepted that from then on the boy's mother would have the right to drop in on them unannounced to make sure there was nothing strange and that Luca was all right.

Now that everything was done and signed, Enzo was allowed to see Luca again. When he honked the horn and the front door of his ex-wife's house opened, when he saw Luca come running toward him, seeing the boy felt like a kind of miracle.

"How are you, champ?" Luca didn't answer. He closed the car door and tossed his backpack onto the back seat. "Glad to hear it," said Enzo, "and you're going to love the new place."

He'd painted the boy's room black, just as Luca had begged him to do a few years before.

"You can write on the walls with chalk," he explained, and Luca muttered that he wasn't five years old anymore.

Though the house was small and there was no yard, they were seven blocks from downtown and Luca could walk to school. He liked that; Enzo even caught a brief smile.

That first week the new apartment smelled strange and it was hard to find things, but they were together, and that was all he'd been fighting for.

The neighborhood real estate company had found some tenants for his house. The new occupants would move in on the first of next month, so if Enzo wanted to salvage any of the containers he'd left in the greenhouse, he had to do it before then.

"You'll also have to leave us your key," said the man from the realty company. "I always forget that part."

Enzo woke up from a long nap, alone in the new apartment, since Luca would still stay at his mother's on weekends. He got up, made some coffee, and decided he would make that final trip to the other house.

It was twilight by the time he arrived. He opened the blinds and turned on the lights. Empty and newly painted it looked bigger and sadder than ever; still, he wondered how long he would last in the new apartment before he desperately needed to come back. He went out to the patio and opened the door to the greenhouse, where, before he'd left some weeks before, he'd set the kentuki in a corner on its charger. And there it still was, motionless, the contact light with the charger still on. He'd thought about the mole many times, regretting that he hadn't thrown it definitively into the trash. Why keep it alive, even after he'd promised to disconnect it? Maybe he just wanted to know. He flipped the light switch and stood awhile looking at the greenhouse's deplorable condition. Some dark, dry tangles drooped from the flower beds toward the floor; a peperoncino had rolled to the middle of the room and was rotting there, moldy and alone. Then he heard the phone. It was ringing inside the house. He dropped his bag to the floor and left the greenhouse, crossed the yard, and went in through the kitchen. He stood for a moment looking at the old wall phone; it was the only thing that had been in the house the day he and Luca moved in, and the only thing that remained the day they left. It was old and outdated, and still it kept on ringing. He picked up the receiver. A rough, dark breathing made his skin prickle.

"Where's the boy?" asked the voice, in English.

Where was his son? For a moment he wondered if something hadn't happened at his ex-wife's house. He made an effort to keep the receiver pressed to his ear. It was the other man's breathing, coiling into his body, that helped him understand.

"I want to see Luca again."

Enzo squeezed the receiver so hard against his ear that it hurt.

"I want . . ." said the voice. Enzo hung up.

He hung up with both hands and then he couldn't let go of the phone. He stayed like that, hanging on to the device as it hung from the wall. Then he looked around the empty living room and forced himself to breathe, thinking about the possibility of sitting down but unable to actually make any movement, reminding himself that no one was watching him, that the kentuki was still on its charger, locked in the greenhouse.

When the phone rang again, he leapt back and stood looking at it from the middle of the kitchen, frozen, until he made a decision. He left the house and entered the greenhouse. The kentuki was waiting for him on its charger. Enzo opened the closet where the tools were stored and took out the shovel. He climbed into a flower bed, pushed aside the dry plants on the surface, and started to dig. Making an effort not to turn his head, he sensed the kentuki get down from the charger and roll away. It couldn't escape; before he'd gotten the shovel, he'd made sure to lock the door. He dug until he thought the hole was big enough, then threw the shovel aside and approached the kentuki. The mole tried to get away, but Enzo had no trouble catching it and picking it up. Its wheels spun desperately, turning to one side and then the other. He laid it down in the little grave, faceup. The mole turned its head back and forth, now unable to move its body. Enzo dragged the mounds of dirt from around the pit to cover the sides of the body, the belly, and most of the head. He threw the rest of the dirt over the eyes, which never closed. He pummeled the earth with his fists, with all his strength, until he heard something crunch, crunch and yet tremble, move imperceptibly. He picked up the shovel again, raised it in the air and pounded it against the earth. He brought it down again and again, compacting the dirt until he was sure that even if a living being still throbbed beneath it, no crack would open up again.

Oaxaca

· ·

THEY DRANK ONE FINAL COFFEE at the kiosk.

"When are you leaving?" asked Carmen.

"Sunday," she said, and she realized Carmen was the only person she'd told that she was leaving early, though she hadn't mentioned exactly when. Nor had she found the right moment to tell Sven.

"You're leaving me alone in this hell, *manita*," said Carmen, and she finished her coffee in one gulp.

They hugged. Alina thought how much she would miss her—in the end something good *had* come from this time in Vista Hermosa. They crossed the zócalo together and said goodbye in front of the church. Alina went back, arming herself with patience. It seemed like the perfect afternoon for a lot of things, but the *artiste*'s great opening awaited her at the Olimpo.

Sven had been holed up in the main gallery for a week, working with his assistant. His Catalan gallery reps had hired a photographer to document the whole installation process, and since then Sven and the kentuki had practically disappeared. These past few days Colonel Sanders hadn't even come up to the room to see her. He'd stayed in the studios until after dinner, socializing in the common areas, maybe even with other kentukis. Sven had definitely abandoned his mono-prints, and expectations for the installation were growing, but Alina didn't have the slightest idea what it was the *artiste* was plotting.

She found the parking lot full of cars, and two taxis pulled up one behind the other to drop off another handful of visi-tors. Although it wasn't dark yet, the lights of the residency grounds were already on. Moving through the flood of strang-ers, she wondered what time it was. Near the gallery she stopped in front of her reflection in a window and smoothed her hair. She also straightened her sundress, adjusting the straps that came up from the waist and tied behind her neck. As she did she noticed that those nearly two months of daily runs had worked wonders on her body.

On reaching the top steps she heard a wave of applause— she was late. She imagined Sven standing next to his assistant, trying to contain his satisfaction. No one ever clapped like that for the *artiste*'s gray monoprints. She dodged a few people and entered the central hall of the gallery, where several wait-ers were serving champagne. The show began farther in. She went into the first room, where the audience was dispersing. On one of the walls, a large photo of Sven crowned his biog-raphy. Sometimes she forgot how handsome he was; she was thinking about that when she realized something strange: there was nothing hanging on any one of the four large white walls. Not a single artwork. There were kentukis everywhere—

in fact, there was an owl at her feet, studying her. The floor was covered in violet plastic circles, and each circle contained words: *touch me, follow me, love me, like me.* And also *donate, photo, enough, yes, no, never, again, share.* She realized she was standing on a *come closer* and the kentuki that was looking at her was on a *call me.* It had a phone number written on its forehead; in fact almost all the kentukis had something written on them: numbers, e-mails, names. They also had papers stuck to their backs: *I'm Norma and I'm looking for a job; We're a nonprofit organization, and by giving just €1* . . . Some of them bore photos, dollars, business cards, tasks. The kentuki at her feet squeaked and spun around on its *call me* circle, and Alina looked around for a nearby *no*, but the two she found were occupied. There seemed to be as many people as there were kentukis, and together they were composing an interminable sequence of squeals, phone conversations, and erratic jumps from circle to circle. It was too much. One man raised a *give me* into the air and turned from one side to the other, like the girls who show the numbers in a boxing ring.

"Have you seen a *never?*" one woman asked her.

She was holding against her chest a dozen *never*s that she must have been collecting. Alina shook her head, gave a jump when she realized she was standing on an *I love you*, and moved again to get away from a *touch me* and an *I want.* But there wasn't enough space to say nothing, she was always stepping on something. She fled to the next room.

"It's so cool, right?" said a feminine voice as she passed.

Alina turned. It was the assistant, who winked at her before walking off toward the hall. Did the girl know who she was, then? Would she know where Sven was? By the time she started to ask, the assistant was gone.

The second room was smaller and had fewer people in it. In the center, a wooden pedestal held a single kentuki, as if it were a totem. It was a rabbit. Alina went closer to the two screens that were on the wall. Right away she understood that they were the two past faces of that poor rabbit kentuki, rigid and extinguished on its pedestal. On the first screen, a camera moved between the legs of the chairs in a dining room, close to the floor. The screen next to it seemed to be the reverse angle: a man was looking into the camera and working on a keyboard. Had Sven communicated with that user in advance, asked him to place a camera in front of him? Or had the user recorded himself of his own accord, and the material had reached Sven some other way? The man's eyes were moving from one point on the image to another, sometimes glancing down at the keyboard as he murmured something softly. The camera was now crossing a hallway. There was something dirty, lascivious, in the man's manner. He pushed open a door and hid under the bed. A woman was closing the closet door as she finished undressing. The man whistled and put the phone in front of the screen to record it all. Alina imagined herself with Sven in bed, seen from the Colonel's eyes. But she knew none of this could happen to her, she'd been very careful, she'd protected herself from that kind of user since the very first day.

She heard laughter; three more women came in with their glasses of champagne, and Alina moved on to the next room. She was disappointed to find more or less the same thing. Another kentuki in the middle of the room with its screens of keeper and dweller on one of the walls. She didn't stop, but went straight to the next room.

In the doorway she bumped into a man who, after adjusting his glasses, stood looking at her for a moment, clearly flustered. Alina watched him hurry away, bumping into people as he headed back toward the main room. An intuition, vague and dark, made her take a deep breath. She looked into the room. The kentuki had its back to her, but she recognized it immediately. Maybe she'd known even before she went in. Like the other two kentukis, Colonel Sanders was impaled on his pedestal. She recognized the burn on his back, the swastika on his forehead, the beak stuck on his left eye, and his chopped-off wings. His eyes were closed. Then Alina saw herself on the right screen. She watched herself approach the camera in jean shorts and the shirt her mother had given her before she'd left Mendoza. She looked chubbier, but not bad. On the other screen, a man of around fifty years old was looking confusedly at the keyboard. He was robust, with a mustache and sideburns. When a boy of around seven climbed up onto his lap and took the controller from him, the man let him do it and then watched him for a good while, his expression somewhere between tender and surprised at how well the boy maneuvered the kentuki. In the right image Alina moved off toward the bathroom. The boy followed her, dodging the little rugs on the floor and the dresser at the back, but Alina slammed the door on him and the man who held the boy laughed, tickling his stomach. Then the image changed. Now the camera was motionless in front of the closed door of the residency room, and the boy was waiting attentively, stock-still. Behind him, a woman who could have been his mother was putting away a pile of clothes on a shabby shelf. Alina thought about Sven. She couldn't believe it—he'd been watching her the whole time, and all that time he hadn't said a word. On the kentuki screen the door opened, and Alina recognized her own legs and sneakers entering the residency room. On the other screen the boy clapped happily and called to his mother. The images changed again. The man didn't appear for a time, although the boy was always there, crying out in joy every time Alina came on-screen. Sometimes he sat looking at her entranced, a finger up his nose, and once he even fell asleep in front of the screen. Every day he waited anxiously for her to get back from her run, from the library, from sunbathing, from the kiosk, or to simply see her wake up. Alina felt her body tense. Something very strong was pulling her backward, urging her to get out of that room right away, while the images went on changing. She saw herself yelling at the boy through the camera. Showing him her tits. Tying him up so he couldn't reach the charger. Sometimes the boy went running out and the room was empty for a good while. Sometimes the boy was as red as a tomato, his face wet from so much crying even before Alina appeared. Once, the father came into the room and made him turn everything off and come with him. But the boy always came back. He was there watching the decapitations, paralyzed with terror; he was there the afternoon when she hung him from the fan, cut off his wings, and, in front of the camera, set fire to them with the kitchen lighter. He was there the night before, when, bored in bed and not knowing what to do, she had picked him up from the floor and used her lunch knife to stab at his eyes until the screen showed scratches.

Alina took a couple steps back and stumbled against some people who were staring at the images in bewilderment. She had to push them to get by. She went back to the previous room, and the one before that, until she reached the main hall. In the middle, surrounded by admirers, Sven was pointing to a circle on the floor in front of the directors of the residency. Alina stood immobile, breathing roughly. She looked at Sven, saw him smile, accept congratulations, and all she could think about was how much pain she wanted to cause him. But she stayed where she was; she felt so stiff among these people, the circles on the floor, and the whirling kentukis that she felt her body was another piece in the show. Sven had displayed her on her own pedestal; he'd separated all her parts so very delicately that now she didn't know how to move. A tingling prickled over her whole body, even inside, in her chest, and she wondered if she wasn't having an attack: Of nerves, of panic, of rage. Of inertia. She had the urge to scream, but she couldn't. She could only move inside herself, like a woodworm crawling through its own tunnels, digging into an absolutely rigid body. What was her kentuki doing stuck on that pedestal? And how had it been turned off? Had the parents disconnected it? Had Sven asked them to do it, as the finishing touch for his show? Or had it been the boy's decision? She imagined him in his room, staring at his own reflection on the black screen.

She couldn't move, but she could think. If she closed her eyes she saw her Colonel. The burnt metal, the fabric edges singed by fire. She wondered where exactly on the creature's back his shoulder blades would be, and she imagined herself caressing him softly on the hollow between the bones, the way her father used to do with her when she was little. She imagined herself knocking at the door of the boy's house, the boy giving her his hand and letting her lead him to a park down the street. It was a small hand that sometimes squirmed, soft and sweaty, in hers. "We'd better sit down," she was saying, "we have to talk." The boy nodded, and their hands separated as they sat down. The concrete bench was hot from the sun; it warmed their calves tenderly, it gave them time. The boy was attentive, he looked at her, needed whatever it was she had to say. She just had to open her mouth and utter almost anything. But the worm could only drag itself through her inner tunnels, and she was too tired, she couldn't move.

She opened her eyes. The man she'd bumped into earlier as she entered the final room was now walking toward her. She *could* think. She would take a taxi. She'd run up to the car, get in and slam the door, and let the car carry her down the hillsides toward Oaxaca. In the hall, someone pointed to her. One woman looked at her and covered her mouth, as though frightened. Alina told herself that she would hold on tight to the seat of the taxi, that she wouldn't let herself look back. The lights of Vista Hermosa would be lost little by little, until she could see, on the most golden point of the hilltop, only the luminous gallery of the Olimpo. She would forget about all those gods, and putting up no resistance, she'd let herself fall to Earth. She would give in. She told herself this, but she couldn't close her eyes again. She breathed atop the circles, above hundreds of verbs, orders, and desires, and the people and the kentukis surrounded her and started to recognize her. She was so rigid she felt her body creak, and for the first time she wondered, with a fear that threatened to break her, whether she was standing on a world that it was ever possible to escape.

Oneworld, Many Voices

Bringing you exceptional writing
from around the world

The Unit by Ninni Holmqvist (Swedish)
Translated by Marlaine Delargy

Twice Born by Margaret Mazzantini (Italian)
Translated by Ann Gagliardi

Things We Left Unsaid by Zoya Pirzad (Persian)
Translated by Franklin Lewis

The Space Between Us by Zoya Pirzad (Persian)
Translated by Amy Motlagh

The Hen Who Dreamed She Could Fly by Sun-mi Hwang
(Korean) Translated by Chi-Young Kim

Morning Sea by Margaret Mazzantini (Italian)
Translated by Ann Gagliardi

A Perfect Crime by A Yi (Chinese)
Translated by Anna Holmwood

The Meursault Investigation by Kamel Daoud (French)
Translated by John Cullen

Laurus by Eugene Vodolazkin (Russian)
Translated by Lisa C. Hayden

Masha Regina by Vadim Levental (Russian)
Translated by Lisa C. Hayden

French Concession by Xiao Bai (Chinese)
Translated by Chenxin Jiang

The Sky Over Lima by Juan Gómez Bárcena (Spanish)
Translated by Andrea Rosenberg

Umami by Laia Jufresa (Spanish)
Translated by Sophie Hughes

The Hermit by Thomas Rydahl (Danish)
Translated by K. E. Semmel

The Peculiar Life of a Lonely Postman by Denis Thériault
(French) Translated by Liedewy Hawke

Three Envelopes by Nir Hezroni (Hebrew)
Translated by Steven Cohen

Fever Dream by Samanta Schweblin (Spanish)
Translated by Megan McDowell

The Invisible Life of Euridice Gusmao by Martha Batalha
(Brazilian Portuguese) Translated by Eric M. B. Becker

The Temptation to Be Happy by Lorenzo Marone
(Italian) Translated by Shaun Whiteside

Sweet Bean Paste by Durian Sukegawa (Japanese)
Translated by Alison Watts

They Know Not What They Do by Jussi Valtonen (Finnish)
Translated by Kristian London

The Tiger and the Acrobat by Susanna Tamaro (Italian)
Translated by Nicoleugenia Prezzavento and Vicki Satlow

The Woman at 1,000 Degrees by Hallgrímur Helgason
(Icelandic) Translated by Brian FitzGibbon

Frankenstein in Baghdad by Ahmed Saadawi (Arabic)
Translated by Jonathan Wright

Back Up by Paul Colize (French)
Translated by Louise Rogers Lalaurie

Damnation by Peter Beck (German)
Translated by Jamie Bulloch

Oneiron by Laura Lindstedt (Finnish)
Translated by Owen Witesman

The Baghdad Clock by Shahad Al Rawi (Arabic)
Translated by Luke Leafgren

The Aviator by Eugene Vodolazkin (Russian)
Translated by Lisa C. Hayden

Lala by Jacek Dehnel (Polish)
Translated by Antonia Lloyd-Jones

Bogotá 39: New Voices from Latin America
(Spanish and Portuguese) Short story anthology

Last Instructions by Nir Hezroni (Hebrew)
Translated by Steven Cohen

Solovyov and Larionov by Eugene Vodolazkin (Russian)
Translated by Lisa C. Hayden

In/Half by Jasmin B. Frelih (Slovenian)
Translated by Jason Blake

What Hell Is Not by Alessandro D'Avenia (Italian)
Translated by Jeremy Parzen

Zuleikha by Guzel Yakhina (Russian)
Translated by Lisa C. Hayden

Mouthful of Birds by Samanta Schweblin (Spanish)
Translated by Megan McDowell

City of Jasmine by Olga Grjasnowa (German)
Translated by Katy Derbyshire

Things that Fall from the Sky by Selja Ahava (Finnish)
Translated by Emily Jeremiah and Fleur Jeremiah

Mrs Mohr Goes Missing by Maryla Szymiczkowa (Polish)
Translated by Antonia Lloyd-Jones

In the Shadow of Wolves by Alvydas Šlepikas (Lithuanian)
Translated by Romas Kïnka

Humiliation by Paulina Flores (Spanish)
Translated by Megan McDowell

SAMANTA SCHWEBLIN is the author of three story collections that have won numerous awards, including the prestigious Juan Rulfo Story Prize and a Man Booker International Prize longlisting for *Mouthful of Birds* (Oneworld, 2019). Her debut novel, *Fever Dream*, was shortlisted for the Man Booker International Prize in 2017. Originally from Buenos Aires, she lives in Berlin.

MEGAN McDOWELL has translated books by many contemporary South American and Spanish authors, and her translations have been published in *The New Yorker*, *Harper's* and *The Paris Review*. She lives in Chile.

Longlisted for the Man Booker
International Prize 2019

Nominated for a Shirley Jackson Award 2019

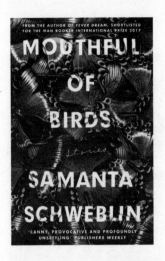

The crunch of a bird's wing.

A cloud of butterflies, so beautiful it smothers.

A crimson flash of blood across an artist's canvas.

Spine-tingling and unexpected, unearthly and strange,
the stories of *Mouthful of Birds* are impossible to forget.
Samanta Schweblin's writing expertly blurs the line
between the surreal and the everyday, pulling the reader
into a world that is at once nightmarish and beautiful.

'Spritely and uncanny, this is a beautifully imagined
and skilfully executed collection of stories.'
Man Booker International Prize Judges

Shortlisted for the Man Booker
International Prize 2017

Selected as a Book Of The Year 2017 by the
*Observer, Financial Times,
Guardian & Evening Standard*

**A young woman named Amanda lies dying in a rural
hospital clinic. A boy named David sits beside her.
She's not his mother. He's not her child.**

The two seem anxious and, at David's ever more
insistent prompting, Amanda recounts a series of
events from the apparently recent past. As David
pushes her to recall whatever trauma has landed
her in her terminal state, he unwittingly opens a
chest of horrors, and suddenly the terrifying nature
of their reality is brought into shocking focus.